ROBIN HOOD

PIRACY, PAINTBALLS & ZEBRAS

D0547811

Robert Muchamore's ROBIN HOOD series:

Hacking, Heists & Flaming Arrows
Piracy, Paintballs & Zebras
Jet Skis, Swamps & Smugglers

Other series by Robert Muchamore:

CHERUB
HENDERSON'S BOYS
ROCK WAR

Standalone novels by Robert Muchamore:

KILLER T
ARCTIC ZOO

ROBERT MUCHAMORE'S
ROBIN HOOD

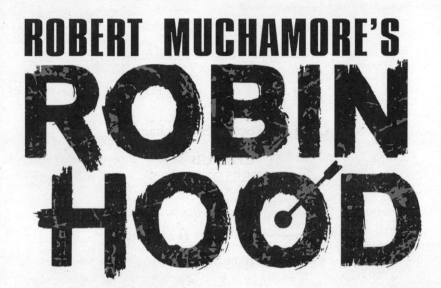

PIRACY, PAINTBALLS & ZEBRAS

HOT
KEY
BOOKS

First published in Great Britain in 2021 by
HOT KEY BOOKS
80–81 Wimpole St, London W1G 9RE
Owned by Bonnier Books

Sveavägen 56, Stockholm, Sweden

www.hotkeybooks.com

A CIP catalogue record for this book is available from the British Library.

ISBN: 978-1-4714-0947-9
Also available as an ebook and in audio

1

Typeset by DataConnection Ltd
Printed and bound in Great Britain by Clays Ltd, Elcograf S.p.A.

Hot Key Books is an imprint of Bonnier Books UK
www.bonnierbooks.co.uk

IRISH
SEA

Liverpool

Lake Victoria

SHERW

Pelican Island (prison)

Nottingham

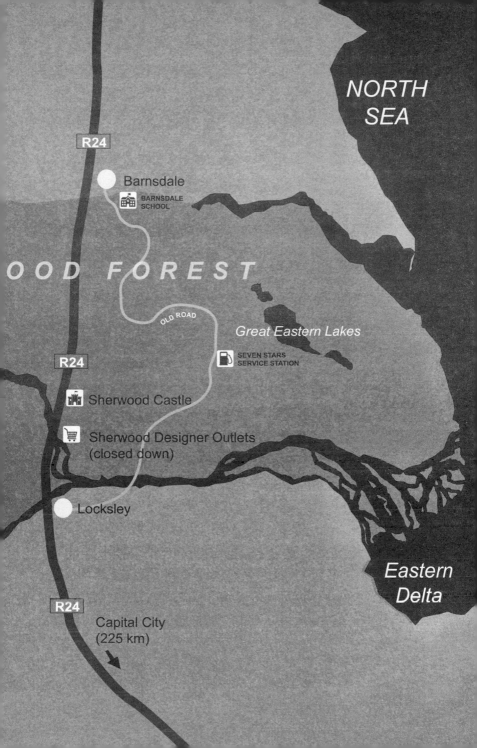

THE STORY SO FAR . . .

It is a time of strife in Sherwood Forest...

Evil gangster **Guy Gisborne** has the declining industrial town of Locksley under his thumb, controlling everything from petty drug deals to senior police and judges.
He works in an uneasy alliance with the Sheriff of Nottingham, **Marjorie Kovacevic.**

The ambitious Sheriff likes to portray herself as a successful businesswoman and get-tough politician, who locks up criminals and cracks down on immigration. But deep in the forest, Sheriff Marjorie has an army of private guards who'll deal brutally with anyone who gets in her way.

But good folks are fighting back!

For more than a decade, **Will Scarlock** has fought to protect the thousands of vulnerable people who live in Sherwood Forest. From a base in an abandoned outlet mall, Will and his comrades provide shelter, healthcare and food to anyone who needs it.

And there's a new hero in town...

When **Ardagh Hood** dared to speak out about corruption in Locksley, Guy Gisborne had him beaten up and framed by corrupt cops.
Nobody expected his twelve-year-old son **Robin Hood** to fight back, but he shot Guy Gisborne with an arrow, staged a daring robbery to raise money for Forest People and took out two Locksley police cars during a citywide riot.
Three months later, Robin is living at the outlet mall, with his new friend **Marion Maid** and her eccentric family.

But Gisborne wants revenge and there's a £100,000 bounty on young Robin's head...

PART I

NEWS UPDATE

'Good afternoon, this is Channel Fourteen serving the Central Region. I'm Lynn Hoapili with your local headlines.

'Our top story is that traffic on Route 24 is still subject to severe delays after a tyre blew out on a truck filled with zebras during this morning's rush hour. The vehicle rolled onto its side and the rear doors flew open as it smashed into the central barrier.

'Eyewitnesses described scenes of chaos as weak and filthy zebras escaped the truck and stumbled into twelve lanes of busy traffic. Several vehicles crashed as they swerved to avoid the animals. Five motorists were taken to hospital by air ambulance and, while most of the animals fled into surrounding forest, vets had to destroy one zebra that was hit by a car.

'A spokesperson for the Animal Freedom Militia has claimed the zebras were being shipped to

Sherwood Castle for an upcoming trophy hunt and that cramming so many animals into a small truck is a serious breach of animal welfare regulations. Sherwood Castle management has so far refused to comment.

'In other news, there has been a surprise twist in the controversial trial of Ardagh Hood. Moments before his case went before a judge, Hood accepted a plea deal. In return for a three-year prison sentence, the Locksley man pled guilty to the theft of laptop computers and to resisting arrest.

'Scuffles broke out when news of the guilty plea reached Ardagh's supporters outside court, and police made several arrests. Hood's lawyer, Tybalt Bull, said he would have liked to continue the fight to prove Ardagh's innocence, but that his client risked a sixteen-year prison sentence if he had been found guilty after a full trial.

'Those are the noon headlines. I'll be back with our main bulletin at one o'clock.'

1. PINT-SIZED TEARAWAY

Sherwood Forest stretched across the land, from Lake Victoria to the swampy Eastern Delta. Twenty thousand square kilometres, inhabited by bears, snakes, gigantic crunchy-shelled bugs and a vast population of yellow birds that lived nowhere else on Earth.

Estimates of Sherwood's human population varied between thirty thousand and a quarter of a million, and most of them were hiding from something. Bandits, bikers, religious cults, terrorists, refugees and one twelve-year-old boy with a £100,000 bounty on his head.

To find Robin Hood you had to travel eight kilometres north from his birth town of Locksley, take a right off the twelve-lane Route 24 expressway, then hike down a road that had mostly been reclaimed by forest until you reached the parking lots of Sherwood Designer Outlet Mall.

It was more than a decade since the sprawling mall sold its last bargain kitchenware and discounted handbags. Now the abandoned H-shaped shopping centre housed a well-organised outlaw community, protected by trip wires, motion alarms and armed guards stationed on a precarious wooden observation tower.

Although it was just after one on a late spring afternoon, Robin Hood had taken to his den on the upper level of an abandoned sporting-goods outlet. The den was eight by six metres, with walls made from wobbly shop partitions. He sprawled face down on a musty but comfortable mattress, buried under oversized cushions, two duvets and a Berber rug.

Robin's bestie, Marion Maid, had been sent upstairs to tell him lunch was ready. She only realised he was under the mound of bedding because a couple of grubby toes poked out.

'Hey, pal,' Marion said quietly, as she knelt by the bed. 'Everyone's about to eat.'

'Don't feel like it,' Robin said.

His words were clipped because he didn't want Marion to hear that he was upset. Normally she'd have dived into the cushions or grabbed Robin's ankle and tickled his foot. But today was different.

'I'm really sorry about your dad,' she said.

'I can't even visit him without getting busted,' Robin complained. 'My mum's dead. And my big brother is living in luxury at Sherwood Castle with his new mommy.'

'You've got me,' Marion said. 'And everyone here has your back.'

Robin didn't respond, so she tried a different tactic. Unfortunately it came out sounding grumpier than she meant it to.

'What are you gonna do? Stay under that mound of covers for the rest of your life?'

'I can try,' Robin snapped back.

'If you can't face everyone, how about I bring a plate up? This afternoon we can watch a movie on Netflix. Take your mind off things.'

'Internet's down,' Robin said. 'And there's *nothing* to do. I'm totally bored and I'm not allowed out of the mall.'

'What are we supposed to do? With a hundred-thousand bounty on your head, every scumbag in Sherwood Forest will be after you.'

Marion watched the mound of covers shift slightly. Dust billowed as the rug slid onto the floor and she smiled as Robin sat up, sweaty and shirtless. His eyes were gluey from crying and his hair was even messier than usual.

'What's funny?' Robin asked, as he stretched and yawned.

'You look adorable,' Marion teased, as she spotted Robin's T-shirt on the floor and flicked it towards him. 'Like a lost puppy.'

'I'm actually kinda starving,' Robin admitted, a bit more cheerful as his head popped through the neck hole of his shirt.

'You're always starving,' Marion said.

'Growing boy,' Robin said, slapping his belly, then creasing up his nose. 'Why do you stink of fish?'

'Went fishing with my cousin Freya,' Marion said, as she sniffed her hoodie. 'Must have got splattered when we were gutting them.'

Robin looked sour as he stood up. 'Thanks for inviting me.'

'We didn't invite you cos you can't leave the mall without guards,' Marion said, as Robin pulled on wrecked Vans.

'I can't hack another week sitting around here, with nothing but schoolwork and your aunt Lucy's sudoku books,' Robin said. 'I need an adventure – like busting my dad out of jail.'

Marion laughed. 'We're twelve, and Pelican Island is the most secure prison in the country. So ten out of ten for ambition, but a fat zero for practicality.'

'So I sit around here, getting older, doing nothing?'

'We get bossed around by grown-ups, do boring schoolwork and try to have fun when we can,' Marion said. 'That's basically what being a kid is.'

'Who wants to be an ordinary kid?' Robin asked determinedly as he grabbed the carbon-fibre bow hooked on the wall beside his bed. 'I'm not ordinary, I'm Robin Hood.'

Marion cracked up laughing as she opened the den's wobbly wooden door.

'What's funny?' Robin asked.

'You,' Marion laughed. 'You're *so* full of it!'

2. NINJA THROWING STARS

Robin's half-brother, John Hood, was at school and heard about his dad's prison sentence when he checked his phone at the start of lunch.

The immense sixteen-year-old was angry that Ardagh had been framed by corrupt cops. But he knew taking a three-year plea deal was better than the sixteen years his father would have risked by going to trial. Especially at Locksley Central Court, where the judges were as crooked as the cops . . .

But the news had thrown John off-kilter. He'd forgotten to grab the books he needed for afternoon lessons from his locker and now he was rushing upstairs to fetch them before the bell went.

Pupils weren't supposed to go upstairs during lunchtime. Most staff just sent you back down if you got caught. But occasionally they'd dish a detention, so John stopped and listened when he heard scouring sounds at the top of the stairs.

After a few moments, he heard voices over the scrubbing. Once he was sure it wasn't staff, he carried on to the top and found a pair of Year Eight boys, who were getting punished by being made to spend lunchtime cleaning graffiti.

They'd been tasked with removing a two-metre orange arrow, with *Robin Hood Rules* written above. Although the boys had been working all lunchtime, they'd only made half the arrow and the ROB of Robin blurry, at the expense of soggy trousers and orange streaks down the wall.

The pair looked sheepish when they saw John Hood's bulk come around the top of the stairs.

'You're his brother,' one, who had curly red hair, said.

'Little John,' the other added, as he sploshed his scouring pad into a bucket. 'That's what they call you, right?'

'Because I'm so small,' John said, irritated by three things at once.

First, John found it absurd that his annoying kid brother had become a hero after shooting local crook Guy Gisborne in the balls with an arrow, staging a robbery and taking out two Locksley P.D. cruisers during a riot.

Second, John was shy and didn't like talking to random people.

Third, he was in a rush to grab stuff from his locker and get to his afternoon lesson in the science block on the opposite side of the school.

'Robin's a legend,' curly said, reaching towards John for a fist bump. 'I hope he's safe, wherever he is.'

'I'm not in contact with him,' John said, as he unenthusiastically bumped the younger boys' soapy fists. 'Hopefully he's somewhere safe . . .'

He was drying his hand on his trousers when he rounded a corner and almost walked into Clare Gisborne and two hangers-on. The pair were big enough to intimidate every pupil of Locksley High apart from John Hood.

'Little John, welly, well, well!' Clare Gisborne said cheerfully.

Clare was in John's year. She was as tough as any boy. An expert martial artist, daughter of the villainous Guy Gisborne and the person John Hood least wanted to meet in an empty school hallway.

'Just heading to my locker,' John said, pointing into the distance.

Clare copied John's booming voice, but slurred the words to make him sound dumb. 'Headinggg toooo mai lockahhhh.'

Her two goons laughed as they squared up beside her.

'Hear your daddy's on his way to Pelican Island prison,' Clare said. 'And little Robin won't last with that bounty on his head.'

John took a step back and held out his hands to show he meant no threat. Clare matched him with a step forward, then pulled up her purple Locksley High polo shirt, revealing tight abs and a holster with pouches for six razor-sharp ninja throwing stars.

'Like my new toys, Little John?' Clare asked, as she raised a single eyebrow. 'How's your footwork?'

She whipped a ninja star from the belt and threw it. One sharp tooth dug into the floor in the spot where John's toes had been a quarter-second before.

'You move well for a big guy,' she said.

John hopped again as a second ninja star spiked the linoleum. As he turned to run, Clare sprang, hooking his ankle and making him sprawl face first over the floor.

The two goons cut around, blocking his escape route. As John rolled onto his back, Clare pulled out another ninja star, squatted down on her haunches and cracked a nasty grin.

'Who's a big boy then?' Clare teased, as John glanced about frantically, trying to find a way out. 'So many targets!'

3. THE LUNCHTIME POSSE

Marion clanked down the sports store's dead escalator behind Robin. They found her family dining at a pair of folding tables pushed together outside their den. Marion's mum Indio was placing a large baked fish on the table, reaching between her partner, Karma, and their just turned three-year-old, Finn.

Marion's brothers, seven-year-old Otto and nine-year-old Matt, had decided to fight over a bowl of rice, even though there were enough dishes on the table to feed fifty.

There were also two guests. Marion's cousin and fishing partner Freya Tuck was no surprise, but her seventeen-year-old half-brother Flash was.

Flash was boy-band handsome, with curly blond hair, dressed in boots and filthy biker denim. He had the patch of the Brigands Motorcycle Club on his back and a studded leather belt with a hunting knife strapped to it.

'Wassup, little dude?' Flash asked, as he gave Robin a high-five.

'What are you doing here?' Robin asked back.

'Incident at the Brigands' camp,' Flash said sheepishly. 'I'll be staying here till my dad calms down and stops threatening to drown me in the sewage pit.'

Marion and Flash's dad Jake was known as Cut-Throat. He was the leader of Sherwood Forest's most notorious biker gang and definitely not a man you wanted to get on the wrong side of.

'Did you get another girl pregnant?' Freya teased, cracking a wide grin.

Otto and Matt started laughing wildly, making rude sex gestures with their fingers, as little Finn asked what *pregnant* was.

'Pregnant is when you have a new baby in your tummy,' Freya explained. 'Like your mummy Karma does right now.'

'Just when I thought my big brother couldn't get dumber, he's exceeded my wildest expectations,' Marion said, swelling with fake pride.

Flash shook his head and tutted. 'What do you know, titch?'

'Oh, *I* know,' Marion said. 'I spoke to our dad on the phone.'

Marion enjoyed having the whole table's attention and paused dramatically.

'They had visitors from another bike gang at the Brigands' camp,' she explained. 'Flash starts playing poker with them and loses all his money. But instead of quitting, he snuck into Dad's camper and stole the Run Fund.'

Robin looked confused as he dragged a chair up next to Flash. 'What's a Run Fund?'

'Runs are when bikers from all over the country meet up and party,' Marion explained. 'Bikers are usually broke, so my dad collects twenty quid a week from everyone in the gang. That way there's money set aside for gas, hotels and bailing people out of jail.'

Freya was shaking her head and gawping as she asked, 'You stole savings from those mad bikers?'

'Kind of . . .' Flash admitted. 'I'm good at poker. Those guys *had* to be cheating!'

'He lost five thousand,' Marion said dramatically. 'Flash only made it out of the camp with all four limbs attached because our dad is gang leader and everyone respects him.'

'It's no big deal,' Flash said, though his body language didn't convince anyone. 'I'm working on a scheme to pay everyone back.'

Marion snorted. 'With your massive brain . . .'

'Shut up for once,' Flash said irritably.

Robin felt sorry for Flash, but Marion seemed determined to score points off her big brother.

'You're not even a good poker player,' she teased. 'I *always* beat you.'

Flash lost his cool and reared up. 'I let you win because you're Little Miss Tantrum when you lose.'

Marion was a sore loser, and Matt chimed in. 'Marion started bawling last week when I kicked a football in her face.'

Otto erupted with laughter as Marion skimmed a boiled potato across the table at Matt's head. Robin thought the entire Maid clan was about to kick off, but Indio shocked everyone by lifting the big wooden salad bowl and banging it down hard.

'Don't you dare throw food, young lady!' she yelled at Marion. 'Can't you lot be civil for the half-hour it takes to eat lunch?'

Everything went awkwardly quiet. Just sounds of cutlery, as Robin grabbed a plate, then chunks of bread and a scoop of cheesy pasta. As he settled back to take his first mouthful, Robin felt Indio's hands rest on his shoulders from behind. She had lots of big goth-style rings and leather bracelets.

'Doing OK, pal?' Indio asked.

'Sorry 'bout your dad, Robin,' Flash added, talking with his mouth full.

Robin felt loved as he looked up at Indio, then at all the others around the table. Out of all the people in Sherwood Forest, he'd been lucky to get taken in by this lot.

'I'll live.' Robin sighed. 'I wish my dad had gotten off, but it would have been risky going to trial.'

'More like suicidal,' Freya said. 'Gisborne has *all* the judges on his payroll.'

'We'll bring down that corrupt scumbag someday,' Karma said, trying to brighten the mood.

'Hear, hear!' several people agreed.

'And we're here if you ever feel sad and want to talk,' Indio said, before leaning in and giving Robin a kiss on the forehead.

Robin was touched, but desperate not to look tearful in front of tough-guy Flash, with his filthy biker gear and giant muscles.

Matt began a story from across the table. 'I watched this documentary about Pelican Island,' the nine-year-old said. 'It's the most brutal prison in the whole country. And, like, there are *vicious* bullies. If you're weak, they steal your money and shoes. And they showed this fight, where this guy got his ear cut off and there was *soooo* much blood!'

As Robin almost choked on cheesy pasta, Marion shot laser eyes at Matt.

'Matt,' she snapped. 'If you're not careful, I'll make a documentary called *Brother Gets Boot Up Backside for Being an Insensitive Dick.*'

Indio glowered at Matt. 'And who let you watch a documentary where a man gets his ear chopped off?'

'I . . .' Matt spluttered. 'YouTube. I clicked by accident . . .'

As Matt continued to squirm, Flash spoke quietly to Robin.

'Your old man's got no worries. The bikers are one of the toughest gangs inside Pelican Island. My dad has sent word and Ardagh will be looked after. Practically a VIP.'

Robin grinned with relief. 'Really?'

'Really,' Flash agreed.

4. SHE WOULDN'T, WOULD SHE?

The viciously sharp throwing star in Clare Gisborne's hand caught sunlight coming through the locker-lined hallway's skylights. Maybe she didn't have the guts to really hurt John, but he didn't fancy sticking around to find out.

Black school sneakers squealed on the floor as John shot up. He feared a metal spike in the back of his head as he bowled Clare's goons out of the way. One tripped him up, but regretted it when John swung an elbow, catching him under the chin and knocking him cold.

The second goon couldn't match John once he was up to speed, but Clare was a lightning bolt. The bell signalling the end of lunch rang as she unleashed her third ninja star. John sensed it whistling through the air behind and dived forward.

The blade skimmed his backpack at a narrow angle, making it ricochet up to the ceiling. The spinning metal smashed into a fluorescent light tube, showering John with glass shards and white phosphorous powder as he skidded along the floor.

Clare had too much momentum to stop. She stumbled into John's legs, slid into a bank of lockers and painfully smashed her shoulder into a drinking fountain. As Clare grabbed another ninja star and turned head over heels back onto her feet, John scrambled towards the staircase, passing the two gawping graffiti cleaners.

John had matched Clare on the straight corridor, but she was nimbler on the stairs. He almost flattened a little Year Seven kid as he rounded the landing. Then, realising Clare was close enough to throw another star, he vaulted the metal stair rail and dropped two metres into Locksley High's main entrance hall.

It was now half a minute since the end-of-lunch bell. Kids were streaming up the ramp from the schoolyard and heading for their first afternoon lesson.

Leaping the banister was genius. Clare was running too fast to copy John's move, and by the time she reached the bottom of the stairs, he'd ducked into the purple mass of Locksley High polo shirts.

'Move!' Clare boomed at the kids in her way when she finally spotted John.

But too many people were trying to get up the stairs, and John was moving swiftly and keeping low to disguise his height. Some smaller kids jumped out of Clare's way, but one Year Thirteen girl didn't like being bossed.

'Do you know who my father is?' Clare snarled, as the girl blocked her path.

'We're not scared of you, Gisborne,' the girl said, hands on her hips.

As several mates backed the older girl up, Clare noticed badges on her school shirt that read *End Police Corruption NOW* and *Robin Hood Rules!*

'Nose in the air like Lady Muck,' one of the girl's friends added. 'You're nothing special.'

Clare could no longer see Little John moving through the mass of backpacks and purple shirts, and this made her furious.

'Just wait,' Clare said. 'See what the cops do to scum like you, with your spray paint and protest badges.'

Kids pouring in from the yard stopped to watch the face-off at the bottom of the stairs, and bodies now gridlocked back to the main doors. A pair of teachers had arrived and were yelling at kids to keep moving and use the other staircases as they tried to wade through.

When the teachers got close, Clare slipped the ninja star into the pocket of her shorts.

'What's going on here?' one teacher yelled.

Clare felt threatened and stepped back up to the stairs.

'They won't let me by,' she said, putting on a good-girl voice.

'Clare was going after Little John,' a younger boy yelled. 'Search her! She's got some knife thing in her left pocket.'

The surrounding kids jeered and shoved. The teachers weren't strong enough to hold everyone off and Clare's stomach churned as the crowd forced her back up the staircase.

'Get to class, the lot of you!' a third teacher on the scene yelled, as he waved a blue pad of detention slips in the air. 'Before I start writing names on these!'

This threat was good at dispersing onlookers, but the older crowd at the bottom of the stairs didn't budge. Two flights up, the pair of graffiti cleaners now had a clear view down at Clare on the first-floor balcony.

One lad picked up his bucket.

The other slowly shook his head. 'We'll be in *so* much trouble,' he pleaded.

'Clare bullied me every day in Year Three,' the kid said bitterly. 'Bent back my fingers and flushed my *Avengers* pencil case.'

He tilted the bucket and let the cold, paint-stained water pour down on Clare Gisborne's head. As Clare screamed and cheers erupted from the crowd, his friend figured, *What the hell*, and dumped his bucket too.

5. SWIRL CAKE STITCH-UP

Karma brought out a frosted raspberry swirl cake for dessert.

'I should eat here more often,' Flash told Robin, as the pair forgot their troubles and tucked into huge slices.

Across the table, Matt and Otto wolfed down cake and dived out of their chairs with hamster cheeks. They'd almost escaped into the mall's main arcade when Indio called them back.

'Where do you two think you're going?'

'Play,' Otto said. 'Meeting the lads at the food court.'

'Don't think so,' Indio said, pointing inside the den. 'You know the rota. Go help Karma wash the dishes.'

'Whaaaat!' Matt complained, staggering backwards as if he'd been shot.

'Are we slaves?' Otto said. 'What about my human rights?'

Marion poked her tongue out as her brothers scraped their sneakers back inside the Maid family den.

'I've got to go on reconnaissance,' Indio told the table.

'For what?' Robin asked.

'Besides feeding and stopping you kids from murdering each other, I'm the local leader of the Animal Freedom Militia,' she explained. 'Will Scarlock has had a tip-off from a source inside Sherwood Castle saying that Sheriff Marjorie is planning a major trophy hunt. We don't know the exact date, but that truckload of zebras on Route 24 means it has to be soon.'

'I saw that before the news about my dad,' Robin said curiously. 'Isn't hunting in Sherwood dangerous?'

'Sheriff's guests don't hunt in open forest,' Indio explained. 'There's a ten-thousand-acre game reserve fenced off behind Sherwood Castle.'

'It's vile,' Freya added. 'They cram the reserve with exotic animals. Giraffes, zebras, big cats, ostriches. When I go fishing with Marion we eat everything we catch. But this is senseless. Hundreds of animals set loose so that rich people can shoot them for *fun*.'

Robin nodded thoughtfully. 'Those zebras on the news looked half dead.'

'That's typical,' Freya sighed. 'Sheriff Marjorie buys cheap animals from dodgy breeders, and conditions in the animal sheds at Sherwood Castle are cramped and filthy.'

'So Freya and I are going to team up with a couple of Designer Outlet guards, head to the edge of the hunting grounds and launch a camera drone to see what's going on inside,' Indio said.

Marion almost shot out of her seat. 'When did we get a drone?' she asked excitedly.

'We're borrowing one of the drones Will Scarlock uses to patrol the mall perimeter,' Indio explained. 'He wants to know what Sheriff Marjorie's up to as much as we do.'

'Why does Will care?' Robin asked.

Marion cut in. 'Sheriff Marjorie wants to boot out refugees, put us Forest People in resettlement camps and use Sherwood Forest to earn fat profits. Everything Will has set up here at Designer Outlets makes life easier for the people she hates.'

Indio nodded. 'Sheriff Marjorie is an elected politician. She'd get horrible publicity if she sent her Castle Guards to clear a peaceful community out of this mall. But she'd boot us out in a heartbeat if she could get away with it.'

'I'd like to see them try,' Flash laughed, as toddler Finn climbed onto his lap. 'Will's guards are armed to the teeth!'

'Can I come along?' Robin asked hopefully. 'I'll be safe if you've got guards with you.'

Freya kissed her teeth. 'Everyone's after the fat bounty on your head, Robbo,' she said. 'What use are two guards if a dozen bandits drop out of the trees?'

Robin sighed. 'But I'm *so* bored.'

Indio smirked. 'Don't you and Marion have maths and history assignments?'

Designer Outlets didn't have a proper school or a qualified teacher, but parents banded together to torture their kids with homeschool courses and work groups in an abandoned bookshop.

'My assignment's almost done,' Marion lied.

'We don't have to submit online until Monday,' Robin added.

'So neither of you has anything to do this afternoon?' Indio asked.

Marion smelled a trap and backtracked. 'Actually, there is still *quite* a lot of work. Robin and me should probably knuckle down this afternoon . . .'

Indio acted like she didn't hear this. 'When I met Will Scarlock to organise the drone, he mentioned that Unai needs help repairing cracks in the roof.'

'Roofing!' Marion squirmed. 'Surely that's not safe.'

Indio laughed. 'It's the flat mall roof you've been running around on your whole life. And don't be stroppy about it. I'm heading out with Freya, Karma needs to rest, and I'd be happier knowing that you and Robin aren't bored and causing mischief.'

'When did we ever cause mischief?' Robin asked cheekily.

'You cause plenty,' Indio said, as she checked the time on her phone. 'So, help clear the table, then get moving. Unai's expecting you by the men's shower block at half past.'

6. PHYSICS CLASS HUBBUB

Once Little John was certain he'd lost Clare, he swept floor dirt off his trousers and made a brisk walk to Physics class. With half the school watching the chaos in the main entrance, he was the first to arrive, though his books were still in his locker and Clare's ninja star had left a huge gash in his backpack.

When the rest of the class finally rolled in, they ignored Mr Kinnear's pleas to settle down and surrounded Little John. There were even kids from other classes who wanted his side of the story.

'Clare chased after me, that's all,' John said.

'Did she have a knife?' a girl said.

Six people spoke at once as the gaggle pushed in and almost tilted John off his stool.

'When the water hit Gisborne! I hope someone recorded it.'

'They dropped paint. Her skin was orange!'

'I almost felt sorry for Clare.'

'Sorry? She broke Tina's arm in soccer last year and got off cos of who her daddy is.'

'Teachers at this school are a joke.'

John hadn't been around to see Clare's fate. 'The graffiti guys dumped water on her?' he gasped.

'Found a video online!' someone shouted.

John wanted to see the video, but he hated being the centre of attention and was relieved when Mr Kinnear waded in, clapping hands over his head.

'If you are *not* in my class, leave! If you *are*, put your bum on a stool and get your books out.'

He walked around, nudging kids towards seats or the exit.

'I'm sure the events of this lunch hour were thrilling,' Kinnear said, as he switched on a whiteboard filled with multicoloured equations, 'but nothing compares to the wonder of physics!'

Little John hadn't made it to his locker, so he shared his neighbour's textbook and wrote on scrap paper. But the class couldn't switch off after all the excitement. The lab rattled with whispers, and loads of kids had phones out under desks.

Just as Physics had finally lulled most students into a stupor, Deputy Head Mrs Bhattacharjee stepped into the classroom and spoke delicately.

'Mr Kinnear, could I *borrow* John Hood for a moment?'

Bhattacharjee was tiny. She always dressed in bright colours, and her hot-pink heels made two clattering steps for each of Little John's strides as they headed for the management-team offices.

Bhattacharjee wasn't one of the tough-nut teachers who dealt with older pupils, so Little John wasn't surprised to find burly PE teacher Mr Barclay when they got to the deputy head's office.

'Sit!' Barclay barked, pointing to a row of trashed sofa units along one side of the room. 'What have you got to say for yourself?'

Little John didn't get into trouble often, but he'd been at Locksley High long enough to know that teachers like Barclay went to town if you didn't stick up for yourself.

'There's CCTV in the upstairs hallway,' John said, trying to sound more confident than he felt. 'Watch the footage. There were three of them, one of me, and I didn't start it.'

Mr Barclay propped his bum on the edge of Mrs Bhattacharjee's desk and scratched greying stubble.

'All pupils involved in this incident will be dealt with,' Mr Barclay began.

John snorted contemptuously. Barclay pretended not to hear and kept talking.

'The CCTV shows that you weren't the instigator. But I have footage showing you flattening Sam Watson. He's currently at the hospital with a suspected broken jaw.'

'I didn't mean that,' John said.

Mrs Bhattacharjee jumped in triumphantly. 'So, you admit that you attacked Sam?'

'Clare was throwing ninja stars and they were blocking me!' John yelled back. 'I know you want to pin this on me, because you're too scared to call Guy Gisborne and say you're excluding his daughter.'

'John, focus!' Mr Barclay said, thumping on the desk. 'This discussion is about *your* behaviour.'

'I hope you can live with yourselves when Clare winds up killing someone,' John said.

'How other pupils are dealt with is none of your concern,' Mrs Bhattacharjee said.

'If nothing I say makes a difference, I'll say nothing.'

John mimed a zip over his mouth and slumped back on the sofa with folded arms.

Mrs Bhattacharjee spoke stiffly. 'You will be sent home until further notice. The Locksley High School management committee will make a decision regarding your future when it meets next week.'

'We need to contact a parent or guardian to let them know we're sending you home,' Mr Barclay added, as he reached across the desk and pulled an emergency contact form out of John's file. 'But your details haven't been updated since your father was arrested.'

John was no smart mouth. He could take half an hour deciding which pair of shoes to wear and, with his head spinning after the lunchtime craziness, it was only the mention of contacting a parent that made him realise he had an ace up his sleeve.

'I've been living with my mum,' John said.

Mr Barclay reached behind to grab a pen off the desk. 'I'll need a number to call her, and a full address to send out a letter.'

'Sheriff Marjorie Kovacevic, The Penthouse Suite, Sherwood Castle,' John said, as he reached down his backpack to get his phone. 'I don't know her mobile number by heart, but it's saved in here.'

Mrs Bhattacharjee seemed sceptical, but Mr Barclay had taught John PE since Year Seven and knew he wasn't a kid who'd make stuff up.

'How can Sheriff Marjorie be your mother?' Mrs Bhattacharjee quizzed, as she closed on John.

'I only found out after my dad was arrested,' John said. 'It isn't a total secret, but my mum has a lot of pull with the local media, so it's been kept quiet.'

The two senior teachers gawped as the news sank in.

While Guy Gisborne was a thug who ran every racket in Locksley, Marjorie Kovacevic was a much bigger fish. Four-term Sheriff of Nottingham, Guardian of Sherwood Forest, senior board member and regional director of the multi-billion-dollar King Corporation. There were even rumours that she planned on moving into national politics and becoming Prime Minister.

As his teachers impersonated statues, John pressed his advantage by tapping the call button on his phone.

'Mum, it's me,' John said, when Sheriff Marjorie picked up. 'I kind of got in a fight with Clare Gisborne.

The school is saying it's all my fault. I'm in the Deputy Head's office and they want to kick me out.'

He put his phone on speaker, then held it out towards Mrs Bhattacharjee, who'd gone wobbly and had to lean against her filing cabinet.

'My mum wishes to talk to you,' John said, stifling a grin.

7. FUN WITH POLYESTER RESIN

Robin acted like he didn't want to do chores, but he'd been stuck in his den all morning and being busy was better than sitting around feeling sad about his dad.

Indio had said they needed to wear long sleeves, full-length trousers and their forest boots for roof repairs, and Robin took his bow everywhere for security. He could load an arrow, aim and shoot accurately in under a second, which is a useful skill when there's a £100,000 bounty on your head.

'It's crowded today,' Robin said, as they joined a small queue for one of the wooden staircases that linked the mall's upper level to the roof.

'Market day,' Marion said.

Designer Outlets' heating and air conditioning no longer worked. So when the weather was decent, mall residents preferred fresh air on the roof. It was also the location of the shower blocks, chicken coops, vegetable gardens, solar panels and stalls that sold clothes, hardware and a dozen types of food.

The mall was protected by armed guards and electronic surveillance. But Monday and Thursday were market day, when outside traders set up stalls and Forest People were allowed in to buy supplies.

After being inside all day, Robin's eyes spent several blurry seconds adjusting to the cloudless sky. It wasn't hot, but the sun had enough kick to let you know summer wasn't far off.

Robin enjoyed market day, with grubby forest dwellers gossiping and haggling over bags of rice or huge packs of toilet rolls. He always lusted after the gear on a stall that sold gadgets and the latest phones, and he usually liked the hot food stalls too, but after today's epic lunch wafts of curry and paella made him queasy.

'Robin!' an elderly French bookseller yelled brightly. 'I saved a book about the Crusades for you. Come and take a look, yes?'

'Later,' Robin said, as he followed Marion. 'I've got chores.'

Before Robin and Marion made ten steps, they found Azeem and her younger sister Lyla standing in front of them. The muscular sisters wore boots and combat trousers and had stun guns and assault rifles.

'You can't be up here on market day,' Lyla told Robin aggressively.

'I'm not in prison!' Robin said, as his eyes rolled with frustration. 'Don't you search everyone for weapons on the way in?'

Azeem sounded more sympathetic. 'If you don't live in the mall, you have to go through security at the main entrance. But we can't check *every* sack of vegetables for a hidden pistol, or open up laptops and solar batteries looking for explosives. So you need to go back to your den.'

'My mum sent us up here,' Marion said. 'We're supposed to be helping Unai with roof repairs.'

Azeem gave her sister a *What do you think?* look, before shrugging.

'Well, if Will OK'd it,' she said. 'But if you're working near the market, let me know and I'll make sure there are eyes on you at all times.'

'Fabulous,' Robin said grumpily. Then, to Marion as they walked away, 'I know they're trying to keep me safe, but I'm going crazy!'

'Life's a bitch, then you die,' Marion said, and emphasised her point by slapping the calf above her twisted club foot.

They found Unai by the showers. The roofer was a chain-smoking Armenian with a scruffy beard and reddish face. His overalls and boots were crusted with dried clumps of grey gloop.

'This roof is a full-time job,' he explained as they headed away from the market towards dazzling reflections from rows of solar panels. 'It wasn't built to hold market stalls and greenhouses, or have hundreds of people walking on it. If I repair one leak, there are two more the next day.'

Unai kept his tools and supplies on a flat-bed wire cart. It held huge plastic drums filled with the gluey resin that was splattered over his clothes, along with paint rollers, brushes and a toolbox that rattled on every bump.

Their destination was the crossing point at the centre of the H-shaped mall. Robin had never been beyond the rooftop market and vegetable beds and couldn't resist peeking through the glass dome, down at the dead fountains and a food court that had once been the mall's centrepiece.

Unai had already marked several cracks in the fibreglass roof with pink X's and began by showing his new recruits how to make a simple repair to the roof's surface.

First he scraped away moss and bird poop from around a crack and roughed up the surrounding area with a cordless power sander.

The repair involved painting the area generously with the gluey plastic resin, then laying a square of plastic mesh on top. After letting this harden for a few minutes, he painted another layer of resin over the mesh.

'Now you try!'

As Unai lit a cigarette, Robin and Marion put on work gloves that were far too big and breathing masks for the resin fumes. Every now and then he'd yell something like, *Paint the resin thick and quick*, or, *Cut the mesh smaller.*

It wasn't exactly fun, but Robin appreciated learning a proper grown-up skill and contributing to the mall's upkeep.

Once Unai finished his smoke, he joined Robin and Marion on their knees and they crawled about until they'd repaired all the marked cracks.

'You've learned the basics,' Unai said, as he began a march back towards the market and signalled for Robin to pull the clattering trolley. 'Our next job is harder.'

8. SHERIFF ON SPEAKERPHONE

Little John set his phone on the deputy head's desk and Mrs Bhattacharjee and Mr Barclay backed up in dread.

'Teachers,' Sheriff Marjorie said, her voice booming confidently from the phone, 'my son, or Gisborne's daughter – who are you going to pick?'

John wasn't a mean person, but the two teachers had been happy to kick him out of school and let Clare carry on running around with throwing knives, so he had zero sympathy now it was their turn to squirm.

'Guy Gisborne and I go back a long way, though relations between us are not always easy,' Marjorie went on. 'I stay clear of his affairs in Locksley, and in return his people keep out of Nottingham and Sherwood Forest.'

The room went quiet, until Mr Barclay asked, 'Sheriff, are you still there?'

'Thinking!' Marjorie snapped back.

It had been less than three months since Little John got blown away by the news that Sheriff Marjorie was his mother. He couldn't decide if he liked his newly discovered parent, let alone loved her. But he had now lived with her in Sherwood Castle for long enough to know that she was extremely clever, and always got her way.

Marjorie Kovacevic had grown up in a care home. She founded her first business while she was still a pupil at Locksley High and became a millionaire in her early twenties when she sold out to King Corporation. She then pivoted into politics, becoming the youngest-ever Sheriff of Nottingham and building a political machine that won her three more terms in office, while she grew richer by awarding lucrative government contracts to her friends.

'Here's what we do,' Marjorie began, when she finally broke silence. 'Locksley High is a terrible school. I'd rather my son was educated privately, but as sheriff, I'm in charge of all the schools in the county and it looks bad if I send my son to a fancy private school while my administration slashes school budgets for everyone else.'

'All my friends are at this school,' John said warily. 'I'm on the rugby team!'

Sheriff Marjorie barely paused. 'Son, a good education is the greatest gift a parent can give, and Clare Gisborne almost killed you with ninja stars. I'd rather avoid a clash with Guy Gisborne, so this is what will happen:

'Locksley High School will issue a letter from the PE department saying that John Hood is an outstanding rugby player who has won a scholarship to another school. If the press finds out, we can say it was a, "Unique opportunity that no parent would deny their son".'

'I'm on the team, but I'm only average,' John pointed out.

Sheriff Marjorie sounded miffed. 'Darling, be quiet and let the grown-ups sort this out . . . Where was I? So, my son gets an excuse to move to an excellent fee-paying school, and you don't have to expel Clare Gisborne. Problem sorted, yes?'

'What about me?' John blurted. 'I have friends, and exams after half-term.'

Marjorie spat words like machine-gun bullets. 'John, if you wish you can have a blowout pool party at Sherwood Castle for all your friends and you'll be the most popular kid in town. And I'm sure Locksley High can arrange for someone to fill out your exam papers.'

John was outraged that someone else could take his exams, but Mrs Bhattacharjee didn't miss a beat.

'Of course, we can do that for you, Sheriff. I'll make sure your son's exam papers are completed by staff and he'll get straight As.'

'See what a good mother I am, John?' Marjorie said. 'Straight A's with no revision!'

'Everyone else has to work for their grades,' John blurted. 'Why should I get a free ride just because you're sheriff?'

'John.' Marjorie sighed. 'Your father, Ardagh, is the most decent and honest man I have ever known. Right now he's flat broke and lives in a filthy prison cell, because that's what the *real* world does to people like him.'

John wanted to stand up and yell, 'Stop, this is all wrong and nobody is listening to me,' but the Sheriff had solved all Mr Barclay and Mrs Bhattacharjee's problems, and his mother spoke *so* fast . . .

'Make sure you erase all CCTV footage of the incident,' Marjorie said. Then finally, 'Call my assistant Mary if you have any more questions. John, I love you and we'll talk tonight over dinner. But now I have to go. I should have been in a committee meeting six minutes ago.'

The phone call went dead and John and the two teachers gasped.

'Such an impressive woman!' Mrs Bhattacharjee said, after a pause.

'Sheriff Marjorie knows what she wants and gets it,' Mr Barclay agreed. 'I hear her staff call her The Tank.'

'Not to her face, I'll bet,' Bhattacharjee laughed.

Little John didn't join the laughter, because he felt like The Tank had just rolled over him.

9. GREASED RAT FANDANGO

Marion sat cross-legged on the end of Unai's trolley as Robin pulled it. They wound up sixty metres from the busy market, where a large section of roof was ponded with stagnant water. Robin noticed globes of golden fat catching sunlight on the water's surface, but while it looked pretty, the smell was like a kitchen bin.

'It's the damned food stalls,' Unai explained, as he puffed on yet another cigarette. 'I've told them a hundred times not to throw fat down the roof drains. But who listens to me?'

Marion and Robin followed Unai into the smelly water and towards the roof's edge. It deepened until it was precariously close to flooding their boots. When they looked over the edge, they saw a half-metre-wide gutter plugged with a gruesome sludge of rotting leaves, cooking fat and litter.

Marion gagged from the smell and flies fizzed into the air as Unai took a hand trowel and probed the smelly brown mass.

'It won't kill you,' he told her with a smile. Then he looked at Robin. 'Fetch my big shovel and the drain rods from the cart.'

Unai did the nasty part of the job. After putting on knee-high wellies, he squelched around the gutter, shovelling sludge into thick plastic bags. It was breezy, so Marion held the bags open while trying not to catch the stench. When each bag was close to bursting, Robin had to carefully carry them through the mini-lake and dump them on the cart.

By the time he'd carried six bags, the rooftop lake was starting to drain. Unai was done with shovelling, and after spraying a strong detergent that would dissolve the remaining fat, he began screwing together a set of bendy drain rods to make a long pole.

Once fitted with a stiff brush, the rods could be shoved into the thick downpipe that led from the end of the gutter to a drain in the mall parking lot.

'It's just puddles now,' Robin said, proud that they'd cleared the huge lake in less than an hour.

Unai aligned the brush with the opening of the downpipe and gave the bendy pole an almighty shove. Marion was horrified as brown water and fat squirted back out of the opening, splattering Unai, with a few drips catching her.

She shot backwards, tripped on a shovel and wound up sat in blobs of fat and foaming purple detergent.

'These jeans are ruined!' she yelled furiously.

But laundry was the least of Marion's problems. When Unai gave the rods a second shove, he disturbed rats nesting on a ledge inside the downpipe. As Marion sat up, she saw three huge rats bounding towards her.

The one that ran over her chest felt warm and heavy, and because they'd spent their lives eating fat in a drain hole, they were slippery and covered in clumps of wriggling maggots.

'AAARGHHHHHHH!' Marion screamed.

She retched as she stood up, but there was fat and grease underfoot, so her boot slipped and she went down again.

'AAAARGHHHHHH!' she continued. 'GET THEM OFF ME.'

Robin had left his bow on the trolley while he was working, but he'd pulled the trolley closer as the lake drained so it was only a few steps away. As the three cat-sized rats splashed through puddles towards the shower blocks and busy market, Robin snatched his bow and a handful of arrows.

The first rat was an easy shot. From less than five metres, he speared its back, pinning the slimy-furred creature to the roof. The second shot was into the sun, twelve metres and running an erratic path. His first attempt grazed butt, but the rat flipped before shooting off again.

His second shot hit the mark and the creature let out wild squeals as it thrashed about, bashing the arrow through its body against the rooftop.

Robin scanned the rooftop for signs of the third rat, but sunlight glinting off puddles made it hard to see and he was sure he'd lost the target, when his eye caught movement in front of the yellow wall of the women's shower block.

The fast-moving target was at the limit of the range an arrow can fly accurately, and pulling back harder to get distance makes aiming more difficult. The rat changed direction as Robin released, but coincidentally his arrow pulled left, hitting the slimy rat face on and skewering it like a kebab.

Marion's screams and the sight of Robin firing arrows had set Azeem and a couple of other guards sprinting out of the market towards them. After throwing down his bow, Robin dashed towards Marion to check that she was OK.

Marion wasn't hurt, but she was soaked through and coated in gunk. Her hair was stuck to her greasy face and her expression was a mix of shock and rage.

'That was exciting,' Robin said sarcastically.

He instantly had Marion's mucky finger wagging under his nose. 'If you *dare* laugh, I'll snap every bone in your body!'

10. LOW ON AMMO

Some people are born organisers and Will Scarlock was one of them. When he'd first arrived at Sherwood Outlets with wife Emma and five kids, less than thirty Forest people lived in the huge abandoned mall.

There was no power, and they either had to lug barrels of drinking water into the forest or risk picking up a nasty bug from the river. Bats and rats had free run of the mall's main arcades and with no security there was a threat of having your stuff stolen every time you went out, or of waking in the night with a bandit's knife at your throat.

Over ten years, Will had restored water and sewage and built a solar farm for electricity. Besides the market, there were chicken runs, vegetable plots, a free medical clinic, mobile phone masts, internet and a library. It was all protected by a watchtower, electronic surveillance and well-organised patrols.

Any desperate soul who came to Sherwood Outlets could get a hot meal and a shower, but you had to pay rent or work if you wanted to stay. Will's rules kept the population a reasonable size, because most people who ended up in Sherwood Forest preferred breaking rules to following them.

Will was in his fifties now, mixed-race, with a chilled persona, terrible teeth and a taste for brightly coloured bandanas. He'd seen some strange things in his decade at Designer Outlets, but now he was jogging away from his rooftop command tent, trying to understand a baffling scene unfolding near the bright yellow shower blocks.

A man had come out of the showers and screamed as his sandal slipped in rat blood. There was Marion Maid looking furious and utterly filthy. There was a half-dead rat with an arrow through it kicking its last, and Unai the roofer yelling at Robin Hood.

'You shot an arrow into my roof!'

'I was aiming at the rat,' Robin shouted back.

'You're supposed to be fixing holes, not making more!'

Looking on were Azeem, several guards and at least thirty market-goers. Some were snapping pics or videoing with their phones, and guards were threatening to ban them from the mall if they didn't delete the footage. It was widely known that Robin had been hiding at the mall, but they didn't want videos being posted confirming that he was still there.

Will stepped in front of Unai and grabbed Robin.

'Azeem,' he yelled, waving frantically, 'take Robin to my tent out of sight. Unai, can you bag the dead rats and hose this blood up?'

'I'm cleaning the downpipe,' Unai said gruffly, then pointed at Marion. 'The girl can do it.'

'What?' Marion yelled.

Will gave Marion a smile and used his most persuasive voice. 'You're already as dirty as you're gonna get. If you clear up, I'll get someone to fetch clean clothes from your den. You can go straight in the shower after, and I'll let you off chores for a week.'

A week off chores for a quick-but-gruesome cleaning job was a decent deal, and Marion was used to gutting fish, so dead creatures and blood didn't bother her.

Azeem was shoving Robin, trying to get him off the scene, but Robin stood his ground and looked back.

'I'm low on arrows,' he yelled to Marion. 'Could you pull 'em out and clean them up?'

Marion growled. 'Anything else, your majesty? How about a back rub and a foot massage?'

'They're carbon-fibre arrows,' Robin begged. 'Ten pounds each. I'll owe you big time.'

Robin wasn't sure if Marion would save his arrows as Azeem put a hand on the back of his neck and started marching him towards the command tent.

'I admire your nerve,' she smirked. 'Anyone asking me to pull arrows out of dead rats would get a bloody nose . . .'

11. GETTING ONE STEP AHEAD

Azeem was on security duty at the market, so she left Robin at the flaps of Will Scarlock's command tent and told him not to go anywhere until Will came back.

The sand-coloured tent hung from tight steel cables between the legs of the mall's watchtower. The inside was dominated by a large planning table. There were two rows of panels showing CCTV footage from around the mall and display boards with dozens of rotas, covering everything from armed security patrols to picking rooftop tomatoes.

Will's wife, Emma, worked at a laptop, while their youngest son, Neo, was up back, fiddling around in a server cabinet.

'You OK?' Emma asked. 'I was sorry to hear about your dad.'

'I'll miss him,' Robin said sadly. 'But what can I do?'

'We were just looking for you,' Neo said.

Neo Scarlock was eighteen and somewhere between a punk and a goth. He wore all black, with his top lip pierced and short bleached hair.

Will stepped back into the tent and smiled at Robin. 'Be *extra* nice to Marion next time you see her,' he warned. 'She's *not* happy with you.'

'I'll make it up to her somehow,' Robin said, then sighed before looking back at Neo. 'You said you'd been looking for me?'

Neo nodded. 'My genius dad sends our number-one computer geek out to repair the roof, while I struggle with this get-up.'

Robin stepped around the planning table and studied the tall server cabinet. There were three rack-mount computers slotted into the cabinet as well as various smaller gadgets, including a powerful encryption device, a box with displays showing the current output from the mall's solar panels and another linked to a spectacular tangle of spaghetti from dozens of CCTV cameras.

On the rug in front of the cabinet was a new 64-port network switch, along with its cardboard box and instructions.

'I've wired this new switch to all the Wi-Fi outlets twice,' Neo explained. 'I've downloaded new firmware, rebooted, switched out cables in case one is faulty. But I'm still not getting an internet connection.'

'I'll have a look,' Robin said, as he knelt down. 'But I'm no networking expert.'

Designer Outlets' internet had died when the network switch blew four days earlier and Robin was keen to make it work.

'You've wired connections to all servers,' Robin muttered to himself, as he glanced at the instruction manual spread on the floor. 'And you've plugged all the cables for Wi-Fi . . . but . . . The internet runs from the optical modem, yes?'

'Sure.' Neo nodded.

'Where is that coming into the switch?' Robin asked.

As Neo looked confused, Robin had a light-bulb moment. He shuffled on his knees and stuck his head into the server cabinet. As hot air from computer fans blasted Robin's face, he reached in the back and fished out a loose orange cable running from the modem.

'You won't get internet if the switch isn't plugged into the modem,' Robin explained.

As Robin plugged in, the switch lit up with dozens of blue and amber lights that signalled data being transferred. Emma tapped something into her laptop and brought up a web page.

'We have internet!' she said triumphantly.

'Not plugging the modem in is *so* embarrassing!' Neo admitted as he facepalmed. Then he took it out on his father. 'I told you Robin should be our IT person.'

'I just plugged a modem into the switch,' Robin said modestly, as he pulled his own phone and logged into the mall Wi-Fi. 'Hacking is more my specialty.'

Will smiled. 'Next time our internet dies, Robin will be the first to know.'

Emma laughed. 'Even if it's 3 a.m.?'

'I was thinking about computer stuff while I was out on the roof,' Robin told Will. 'Indio said you like to know what's going on inside Sherwood Castle.'

Will nodded. 'Sheriff Marjorie is always cooking up some scheme to make life harder for Forest People. A few friendly staff inside the castle tip me off when they catch gossip, but they're cleaners and chefs. Nothing high up.'

'Marjorie's Castle Guards are vicious,' Neo added. 'They killed a bunch of people when they blew up the Sherwood Women's Union compound a few months back. Sheriff Marjorie denied everything and blamed it on bandits, but a tip-off from inside could have saved their lives.'

'One of the dead was a boy younger than you,' Emma added.

Robin nodded solemnly, before saying, 'I might be able to hack into the Sherwood Castle computers.'

Will, Emma and Neo looked ridiculously excited and Robin realised he had to manage their expectations.

'*Might*,' he stressed. 'I can't promise, but Sherwood Castle has a fancy hotel. The computer system must be linked to the outside world, so they can order supplies, take bookings, run guest Wi-Fi and stuff. If one of your sources can get me basic info, like the type of software the hotel uses and a photo inside the server room, there's a chance I can hack their systems.'

'I should be able to get that,' Will agreed.

'I have an account on all the good hacking and piracy forums,' Robin said. 'Once you've given me basic info, I can do some research. I've got time on my hands, so there's no harm having a go.'

'None at all,' Neo agreed, as he exchanged smiles with his parents.

12. ALPHA MALE FACE-OFF

Little John's brain felt like scrambled egg. His dad was in prison, his mum treated him like he was a little kid and while he didn't have heaps of friends or feel massive loyalty to Locksley High School, it had been *his* school for the past five years.

As John walked to his locker to empty it out, he looked through doors at kids sitting in classrooms and felt a touch sad that he'd never do another lesson here, never queue for another lunch, never banter with the lads before a rugby match, never inhale the stench in the boys' toilets . . .

He tutted as he passed the half-scrubbed *Robin Hood Rules* at the top of the stairs. The glass had been swept where Clare's ninja star smashed the light fitting, and his phone rang as he noticed dented metal where she had slammed the water fountain.

John didn't know the number on-screen, but instantly recognised the Israeli accent of Moshe Klein, a burly former special forces officer who headed up Sheriff Marjorie's security team.

'I'm waiting in the car,' Moshe said. 'Stretch Mercedes, parked out front.'

'Won't be long,' John said. 'I've got to clear my locker. The only thing is, I've got a massive hole in my backpack. Do you have a bag or something in the car?'

Moshe hummed for a second. 'I'll take a look in the trunk, then come and give you a hand.'

'First floor,' John said. 'Up the main stairs, turn left, first right then keep walking till you find me.'

'With you in five,' Moshe said.

John pocketed his phone, then got chills as he neared the corner where he'd bumped into Clare and her goons. The grubby vinyl floor had deep gouges where her ninja stars hit, then weirdly he heard Clare's voice.

'Daddy.'

It wasn't Clare's normal cocky tone. More like she'd been crying, and John thought he'd imagined it until she spoke again.

'Daddy, *please* listen,' she begged.

'No, you listen,' Guy Gisborne snarled back at his daughter.

John's heart skipped. If he hadn't paused to look at the floor, he'd have walked straight into Clare's psychotic leather-clad father and his rhino-skin whip.

Guy addressed his daughter furiously. 'I'm ashamed of you. Letting that giant blob escape, then backing out when they confronted you downstairs.'

'There were twenty of them,' Clare said. 'Boys and girls, all older than me.'

'Doesn't matter,' Gisborne said. 'I started you in judo and kick-boxing when you were four. You should have smashed the closest one's nose and gone down fighting if you had to. But you *never* show weakness by backing off. You have to find the names of those boys who dumped water on you and make them regret it.'

'Can't you do it?' Clare pleaded.

'You're the one who lost respect,' Guy said. 'Only you can win it back. And it's lucky you're a girl. If one of your brothers shamed the family like this, they'd feel my whip.'

'It's *different* since the riot and Robin Hood,' Clare complained. 'Everyone hates us.'

John's phone pinged. He gulped and backed up as he read a message from Moshe:

FOUND A BAG, HEADING UP NOW

The ping echoed and Gisborne stepped around the corner to see who was there.

'The giant blob himself!' Gisborne growled.

Clare followed her father, but looked nothing like her usual self. She'd changed from her wet uniform into Crocs and PE kit. Her hair was straggly and her eyes were ringed red, like a normal kid who'd had a really bad day.

'Mr Gisborne,' John said, polite and frightened. 'Just here to empty my locker.'

Gisborne's black leather trousers squeaked, as his hand moved to a hefty whip at his side.

'Lucky for you your mother is somebody important,' he snarled. 'But I won't forget what you've done.'

John heard footsteps behind and was relieved to see Moshe Klein, and the gun bulging under his tweed suit.

'Maybe you should stop picking fights with kids,' Moshe told Guy Gisborne, as he closed in. 'Didn't you get owned by a twelve-year-old the last time you tried?'

'Well, if it isn't Sheriff Marjorie's head monkey,' Gisborne taunted back. 'Here to save the world with Krav Maga and a daft suit.'

'Should have realised that was your absurdly customised truck parked out front,' Moshe said.

'Black Bess Two,' Gisborne said proudly. 'It's got rims that cost more than you'll earn in this year.'

'I'm a soldier not a poser,' Moshe growled, as he closed in to tower over Gisborne. 'While you were squeezing protection money out of shopkeepers and recruiting zit-faced drug dealers, I was jumping out of helicopters. Fighting for real, in a war.'

John was grateful for his back-up, but suspected Moshe and Gisborne would trade insults until sundown if someone didn't interrupt.

'Let's empty my locker and get out of this dump,' John urged, as he took a dark green roll bag from Moshe.

Gisborne looked back at Clare and grabbed her wrist tightly. 'Home!' he barked.

As Clare went towards the exit and John to his locker, they passed within half a metre of each other and exchanged looks that were almost sympathetic. Two teens tangled in an adult rivalry that neither had asked to be part of.

13. MY ONLY WEAKNESS IS TEMPTATION

After cleaning up gore and scrubbing Robin's arrows, Marion decided to treat herself. Besides the mall's basic rooftop showers, a group of Moroccan women ran Arabian-style baths in a former perfume store on the mall's upper level.

Amidst gentle music and flickering candles, Marion stepped into a copper tub filled with steaming water. As she settled in, one of the attendants tossed rose petals across the surface and gently massaged her calves and tired feet.

They added pails of hot when the bath cooled and brought cucumber water to drink. Marion stayed in until she'd shrivelled like a prune and had to pee. After drying with thick towels, she put on white pumps, one of only two dresses she owned and a squirt of Middle Eastern perfume that almost choked her.

When Marion got back to the family den, Indio was still out on the scouting mission and everyone had to be quiet because Finn was asleep. That was no fun, so she scoffed some leftovers from the fridge and jogged up the escalator to find Robin.

'Three scrubbed arrows,' Marion said, when she found him sprawled on a little sofa watching an old TV with a fuzzy picture. 'Be very grateful.'

'Thank you,' Robin said sweetly.

'What's this old telly on for?' Marion asked as she sat. 'I heard you'd fixed internet.'

'Local news,' Robin explained. 'I want to see what they say about my dad.'

A shout of '*Robin*' came from outside the den. It seemed friendly, but Robin still picked up his bow before peeking out of the door and eying Flash.

''Sup,' Flash said shiftily. 'My sister in there?'

Robin nodded. 'Wanna come in?'

'Nah,' Flash said, making a sneaky *come outside* gesture. 'I met this *stunning* girl in the market earlier and I'm heading off to meet up. But I need to ask you something, in private.'

Marion could hear most of the conversation from the sofa and yelled, 'Don't trust my brother, whatever he's after!'

Robin knew Marion was probably right about Flash. But looks, muscle and confidence with girls made him the coolest guy Robin knew and he wanted Flash to like him.

'I'm in a bind with this money I took from the Brigands,' Flash said, as he backed up towards the escalator so that Marion couldn't hear. 'Apparently a couple of them were in the market earlier, asking questions about me.'

'Bad guys?' Robin asked.

'They're all bad when you owe 'em money,' Flash said. 'But I have a plan to earn back the five thousand and a whole lot more.'

'Good for you,' Robin said.

'But I'll need your hacking skills and we'll have to sneak out of the mall overnight.'

Robin looked wary. 'Marion knows the secret mall entrances better than anyone.'

Flash shook his head. 'She's a daddy's girl. Keep her out of this.'

Robin didn't like the idea of going behind his best friend's back, but Flash gripped Robin's shoulder and gave him pleading eyes that he now realised were *exactly* like Marion's.

'Robin, I *need* money before some mad biker puts an axe in me,' Flash begged, 'and you keep saying how bored you are, so this works for both of us.'

Robin half smiled. 'I will go mad if I don't get out of this mall soon.'

Flash took his smile as a *yes* and cracked a grin. 'I *knew* you were cool!' he said. 'It's a three-way split, and you'll get a full share.'

'Three?' Robin queried. 'And you haven't even told me what I'm hacking!'

'The third person is a friend on the inside who told me about the job,' Flash said, as he let go of Robin's shoulder, then checked the time on his phone. 'It'll take a few days to get organised. I've gotta head for this date, but I'll talk you through the details tomorrow. I promise you'll love what you hear.'

'Right,' Robin said suspiciously.

Flash started walking but turned back three steps down the escalator.

'Not a word to my sister,' he warned.

'I'm zipped,' Robin said.

The local news was starting as Robin headed back into his den.

'What did thicko want?' Marion asked.

'Problem with his laptop,' Robin lied. 'He's bringing it here tomorrow for me to take a look.'

PART II

FIVE DAYS LATER

14. THE GREAT ESCAPE

Robin's phone lit up under his bedcovers and he read the time: 00:19. He rolled out of bed, already dressed in a camouflage shirt, black cargo pants and socks tucked into trousers to stop bugs crawling up his legs.

With three raucous brothers and a pregnant stepmum who peed six times a night, Marion had taken to sleeping in the upstairs den with Robin. Robin would never admit that he sometimes got scared at night when he was alone, but he liked having Marion around, apart from now when he had to sneak out without waking her up.

After swinging his bow and a bunch of arrows over his shoulder, Robin hooked his walking boots over his fingertips and crept towards the door on socked feet. Marion had her mattress against the wall behind the little sofa. She'd nodded off while reading, and music fizzed from an earbud that had dropped onto her pillow.

Marion would flip if she found Robin sneaking off with Flash, but if things went to plan he'd be back by sunrise. He tried to ignore feelings of betrayal as he opened the door. There was no squeak, because he'd planned everything out and oiled the hinges the day before.

Robin had been attacked in his den by Gisborne's people a couple of months earlier, so now Indio or Karma put a motion-sensor alarm by the sports store's entrance when they locked up at night. Another sensor pointed down from the top of the escalator, and Will Scarlock had arranged night-time security patrols so that an armed guard was never further than a thirty-second sprint.

These sensors had been the biggest problem with Robin's escape plan, but he'd found another way out. Outside of the den, he crossed to the back of the store's upper level, occasionally flicking a torch to avoid clattering into the scooters and Lego that Marion's brothers left lying about.

A double black door opened into a stockroom, whose shelving racks had once housed several thousand pairs of sports shoes. Robin sat on the floor to put his boots on, then reached up to grab a rucksack he'd stashed there a few hours earlier.

It was a heavy lump, containing his laptop, tools, computer cables, water, chocolate bars and extra arrows that bristled out of the top. Opening the emergency exit onto the fire escape would have triggered an alarm, but there was a large cargo elevator at the back of the stockroom.

It hadn't moved in years, and the inside reeked because Otto and Matt used the open car as a urinal, but Robin had found a service panel in the floor. He'd unscrewed two catches and prised it open with a big screwdriver three days earlier.

When Robin had practised his escape route, there had been chinks of daylight coming from skylights. But now it was night and he peered through the open hatch down an elevator shaft that was pitch black. The cargo elevator only went one storey, but Designer Outlets' shops were built with high ceilings, so it was more like dropping two storeys in a house.

The jump was complicated by the weight of Robin's pack. He didn't want to throw the bag down and risk breaking his laptop, but he could also damage it if he didn't land on his feet. Ideally he would have found some rope to slide down, but he'd only had five days to plan everything, so he'd had to cut corners.

But Robin was a born daredevil, who'd been scrambling over rooftops and running narrow beams almost since he could walk. After making sure everything strapped to his back was tight and sitting with his legs through the slot, he grasped the rim of the service panel and swung himself through.

To minimise the drop, he dangled briefly by his fingertips before plunging into the shaft. With no light the ground came faster than Robin expected. His ankle jarred and one knee touched down, but the only damage was his utility knife dropping out of his pocket. He flicked on his torch and found it on the floor amidst thick dust and the skeleton of a snake.

Robin hadn't managed to budge the elevator doors when he'd surveyed the exit from the outside, but he'd unscrewed a metal panel alongside and now it clanked as he lifted it out. He squeezed through a gap between layers of foam insulation and stepped into outdoor air.

Robin was now on a high kerb, designed so that trucks could back in and unload without needing a ramp. The service road past the delivery bays was a couple of metres below the mall parking, and rust-streaked signs pointed to long-dead shops:

Maureen's Bed & Bath – Bay 126
Chester House Shoes 127
XXX Skate Outlet 128–131

Robin's phone said 00:27. Flash was due at 00:30 but Robin figured he'd get started on the next step of the escape plan.

Security cameras are cheap, but when you're protecting a space as big as Designer Outlets, the system designer must balance the number of cameras with the ability of security staff to watch all the feeds.

Will Scarlock had decided it was better to have thirty-six cameras covering the most important areas of Designer Outlets, rather than the several hundred it would have taken to cover every shop and several kilometres of hallways.

The video output from the cameras wasn't encrypted, so Robin had been able to log into the mall network from his laptop. He'd made sure there was no camera covering the cargo bay behind the sports store, and just one covering the huge expanse of overgrown car park separating the mall from dense forest.

Robin sat on steps at the edge of the steep kerb and pulled out his laptop. The screen lit his face as he logged into the mall network with an administrator password that he'd taken from a Post-it inside Will's server cabinet. He then typed an operating-system command that brought up a list of every device logged into the mall network, from computers and printers, to dozens of phones using Wi-Fi, and the all-important security cameras.

After identifying the camera in the list that overlooked the car park, Robin pasted its details into a protocol diversion program that was a basic part of every hacker's toolkit.

When Robin clicked *run script*, the program made the security camera vanish from the network. It was replaced by a recording Robin had made from the same camera the night before, so, for the next seven hours, anyone watching in the command tent would see footage from the previous day.

After double-checking that everything had worked properly. Robin put his laptop away and still had to wait ten nervous minutes before Flash arrived, covered in lipstick smudges.

'Sorry I'm late,' he said cheerfully. 'Can't keep the ladies off me!'

Robin felt wary as his brain threw up Marion's voice, warning him not to get involved with Flash. But Robin had been impressed with the plan, and he was handling all the technical stuff. All Flash had to do was get him to the location.

'I've dealt with the camera,' Robin said, as he stood up, 'but we could still be spotted by a guard in the watchtower. They've got rifles, so use the tallest weeds as cover and move fast.'

He held out the big backpack.

'Why have I got to carry it?' Flash asked childishly.

'It's got all the gear and you're twice my size!' Robin snapped back. 'And you're late, so we need to get moving.'

15. FLASH WINS AT EVERYTHING (ALLEGEDLY)

Robin had only lived in Sherwood for the three months since his dad got framed by the cops. He found navigating the forest confusing in daylight, and terrifying at night.

But people who'd been there for years were experts, with intricate mental maps that picked out vague footpaths and landmarks such as oddly shaped trees or derelict buildings. If you wanted to keep safe, you also had to avoid hazards such as bears, traps and packs of thugs who'd drop from trees and rob you.

Robin wasn't impressed when Flash arrived late, but his confidence was restored as they marched through forest. While Robin fought to keep the brutal pace, Flash told endless bawdy stories.

Robin heard about fist fights, daring raids, beautiful women and drunken brawls at the Brigands Motorcycle Club camp. He was especially hooked by stories of long-running scraps between Brigands and rival motorbike gangs.

'Biker runs make you feel invincible,' Flash said, as Robin trailed breathlessly. 'We take all our bikes out of the forest and meet up with Brigands chapters from other parts of the country. Two or three hundred bikes roar along the seafront, or through the capital. We make so much noise everyone is scared. Even the cops run away!'

'Your dad kicked you out though,' Robin said.

'They're always broke,' Flash said airily. 'When I rock up with piles of cash, it'll be all hugs and forgiveness.'

As the march went on Robin noticed that in Flash's stories he won every fight, every hand of poker and barely had to look at a girl before she snogged him. But Robin didn't call out the lies, because the stories were funny and took his mind off eight kilometres of tough forest.

Their first stop was an abandoned electricity substation close to Old Road. Robin was intrigued by the rusted cables, bird-poop-splattered capacitors and faded **DANGER OF DEATH** signs with pictures of stick men getting zapped.

Old Road was a meandering north–south route that had existed since Roman times, but power lines and traffic had been redirected when the immense Route 24 highway was dynamited through the forest.

The four-lane road was now controlled by King Corporation, under a highly profitable forest-management contract dished out by Sheriff Marjorie. The company spent as little as it could get away with, leaving Old Road with faded markings, severe cracks from flood damage and poor lighting. They'd also replaced regular Forest Ranger patrols with camera drones.

A battered Subaru pickup with two dirt bikes on the back was parked on low ground beside the substation. It was out of sight from the road and the lights were off, but it wasn't the kind of place where you wanted to be alone after dark. The woman at the wheel was taking no chances, with an assault rifle across her lap.

Flash winked his torch three times. The woman flashed back with headlights then stepped out of the driver's side door.

'Agnes, baby!' Flash said, as he jogged up and gave her a kiss on the cheek.

She was no older than twenty. Dressed in a stiff red skirt and a striped red-and-white blouse with the Seven Stars Petroleum logo printed on the pocket.

'Look at you!' Flash said cheerfully. 'Corporate slave with the polyester uniform.'

Agnes pinched Flash's cheek and pushed him away when she saw the lipstick smears.

'You're such a rat!' she fumed. 'You stink of beer and armpits.'

'I hiked two hours,' Flash said. 'You expect me to smell of roses?'

Agnes made a disgusted grunt. Flash changed the subject by introducing Robin.

She shook Robin's hand and gave a curtsy, like she was greeting royalty. 'The famous Robin Hood!' she said sarcastically.

It was too dark for anyone to see Robin blush, but not so dark that Robin didn't see scarring on Agnes's right cheek. It ran on down her right arm and the back of both hands. He was too polite to ask, but it was over such a wide area that she must have been burned rather than cut.

Flash had moved around to the back of the pickup to check out the bikes.

'These look solid,' he said, as he squeezed a rear tyre.

'It's wiped my whole savings,' Agnes said. 'Two thousand, and I want that back *before* we split the rest of the money.'

'Tested?' Flash asked.

Agnes nodded. 'Circled the paddock behind my house. I'm no mechanic, but they seemed tight.'

Robin felt nervous as he looked at the smaller of the two bikes, which was meant for him. He'd only ridden a few times, and never in the dark.

16. WHO NEEDS HELMETS?

After they'd gone fifteen kilometres north along Old Road, Agnes pulled the pickup in behind a dead burger joint with a caved roof and wrecked kids' playground.

'I'm due on shift at 3 a.m., but sometimes my boss hangs around cashing up,' Agnes said. 'Give it half an hour to be sure he's cleared out.'

Robin helped Flash untie the bikes and roll them gently off the back of the pickup before Agnes drove it away. Flash knew bikes and seemed pleased after he'd checked the brakes and started both engines.

Flash told Robin to get a feel for riding in the dark with a couple of circuits around the burger joint.

'Helmets?' Robin asked, realising he hadn't seen any.

'You only need helmets if you crash.' Flash laughed. 'So don't crash.'

The bike was heavier than the ones Robin had ridden before and it felt scary at first, circling around the parking lot and drive-thru lane with the only light from a puny headlamp. After a couple of circuits Robin started enjoying himself and sped up, but Flash waved him down.

'Your noise is gonna alert any baddies within five clicks,' Flash said. 'We'll ride up slowly. The road is in poor shape. A big pothole can throw a rider off, so stick behind me.'

Robin hadn't heard any traffic on Old Road since they'd pulled in. It felt spooky, riding behind Flash with trees towering over both sides and cats' eyes down the middle reflecting their headlamps.

It only took a couple of minutes to reach their target. Back in the days before Route 24 opened, Seven Stars Services had been a major rest stop halfway through the forest. It had a huge canopy that once covered six rows of petrol pumps. Now, all but three pumps closest to the payment window had been capped off.

The scenic forest-viewing platform was burned out and the restrooms and coffee shop were permanently shuttered. At this time of morning, the large shop was closed and Agnes worked her shift at a till behind a bulletproof service window. There was a big chute alongside so that she could pass out items from the store.

As Robin and Flash stepped off their bikes, Agnes backed away from the window and opened a side door to let them in.

'Bikes OK?' she asked.

'Sweet,' Flash agreed.

'Cameras in here?' Robin asked as he entered.

Agnes pointed towards a service counter which was used in daytime when the shop was open. Robin slid over and found a little hard-drive video recorder attached to the underside of the counter with Velcro.

Agnes had told him the box wasn't connected to the internet, but after blowing thick dust away Robin inspected it carefully for any signs of Wi-Fi before crossing the floor and dumping it in the big backpack.

'Security here's a joke,' Agnes said. 'I've got bulletproof glass in the window, but that door I let you through has a skinny bolt like a bathroom stall. And we've got panic buttons, but the Forest Ranger station is twenty kilometres south and only staffed until 9 p.m.'

'I'll bash up the door so it looks like we kicked our way in,' Flash said, as he opened a fridge and helped himself to a can of Rage Cola. 'You want me to tie you up or something when we're done?'

Agnes snorted. 'I'll tell the cops you were gentlemen and that I did what I was told.'

Robin grabbed a bottle of cola for himself. He was thirsty after the long walk, so he downed most of it in three gulps and belched proudly as he headed deeper into the store.

Beyond the modern counter and fridges up front, the store looked like a place you could shoot a movie set thirty years in the past. Along with sagging shelves filled with car accessories and Sherwood Forest souvenirs, there were ancient slushy and coffee machines, an out-of-order photo booth, a Hipsta Donut cabinet full of dead bugs and a dusty Mario's Melts sandwich counter with signage offering a £2.99 *Halloween Meal Deal* that expired before Robin was born.

Robin was here for the equally ancient QT3.14 cash machine. He squatted down and rapped on the wobbly orange surround that covered the machine's internals.

'How does it look?' Agnes asked.

There was a crash in the background as Flash battered the side door with a fire extinguisher to make it look like they'd forced their way in.

'Looks good,' Robin said. 'There are few of this design left, and they're scrapping them faster since my last robbery got so much publicity.'

'Can you rob newer machines?' Agnes asked, as Flash whacked the door again and whooped like he was enjoying himself.

'It's harder,' Robin explained, as he unzipped the backpack. 'Every cash machine has better security than the previous generation, but there are heaps of smart hackers always looking for new ways to rip them off.'

'The security van came and refilled it this morning,' Agnes said. 'But it's the only ATM in a ten-kilometre radius, so a lot of Forest People come in here and withdraw large amounts.'

'It's good that it's busy,' Robin said, as he turned on his laptop and methodically laid out the tools and cables he needed for the job. 'The busier the machine, the more cash they put inside.'

'You've got a customer!' Flash yelled, as he pulled up the battered door and ducked out of sight.

Robin got to work as Agnes hurried to the service window to sell a driver forty pounds worth of petrol, a large tea and a bag of mints.

17. MARIO'S MELTS MAYHEM

Robin's first step was to strip the cash machine's outer panel. This needed a T-shaped key/lever that had been 3D printed for his last job.

He got a fizz of excitement as he pulled the panel away, catching a warm dusty smell with a hint of burning. The inside looked exactly as he'd expected, apart from a stubby plastic aerial balanced on top of the display unit. It looked like the ones that stick out the back of a wireless router and was held in place with a blob of Blu-Tack. Its bright white plastic looked newer than the rest of the machine, which was over twenty years old.

This wasn't a situation where you wanted surprises, but Robin tried to stay calm. He felt better after he'd followed the wire coming out of the little aerial to the network socket on the back of the PC.

It was the same slot where the other machines he'd robbed connected to the bank, so he figured it was just that the machine was in a remote area and connected wirelessly. Most likely via a satellite dish on the gas-station roof.

The next step was to take out this cable and plug in his laptop. The hack required two steps. First, installing a program that gave him remote access to the aged computer inside the cash machine, then getting the machine to reboot, running hacked software.

The previous time Robin hacked a cash machine, things had been complicated by a citywide riot and cops parked outside. This felt way less stressful, sat calmly on the floor, sipping the rest of his drink as the software installed and Flash watched with hands in his pockets.

'Do you guys want anything?' Agnes asked as she stepped up next to Flash. 'Another drink, or a chocolate bar?'

'I'm good,' Robin said cheerfully.

A few seconds later the cash machine's amber screen flickered back with a screen that read:

FREE MONEY!
<<< Yes   No>>>

'Gotta love that!' Flash yelped, slapping Agnes on the back and jumping so high he almost headbutted ceiling tiles. 'Money, money, money!'

'You're a little genius,' Agnes told Robin. 'How can you get it to do that?'

Robin shrugged humbly. 'The genius is the guy who discovered the vulnerability and cracked the operating system. I just downloaded two apps and a copied a bunch of instructions from a hacking forum.'

'Pity there's so few of these old machines left,' Flash said. 'We could have a crime spree!'

Robin reached up to the screen and pressed the button next to the **Yes** option. There was a mechanical thunk as the armoured door of the cash box unlocked.

All three of them leaned in for a closer look. Inside the heavy door were four grey plastic trays. They were like the paper trays that slot into a printer or photocopier, except they fitted banknotes. Robin could without having to take it out see that the bottom tray was empty, but when he tugged the next one up it felt reassuringly heavy.

Robin saw fifteen centimetres of tightly packed twenties as the drawer slid out. But after that there was a shiny plastic bag with neon-pink liquid inside, like a giant laundry pod. The horrific realisation of what he was looking at took Robin a tenth of a second, but he'd barely turned away and was spitting the D in a shout of *dye pack* as it exploded.

The pouch of sticky liquid had a fast-acting sodium azide explosive in the base, like the airbag in a car. As a deafening alarm erupted inside the machine, Robin was thrown forward and slapped in the back and cheek by a blast of pink liquid.

Agnes and Flash were close enough to get a thinner, full-frontal mist as Robin sprawled out over the grubby floor. One eye burned with dye and he was deaf in his left ear. The explosive had also been hot enough to trigger a sprinkler head in the ceiling.

'What was that?' a new voice shouted. 'What happened?'

Half deaf and half blind, Robin rolled onto his back to see what was going on. Two women dressed in camouflage and holding guns had sprung from behind the Mario's Melts counter. At the same time, Agnes had pulled a small stun gun taped to her leg beneath her skirt and used it to zap Flash with 10,000 volts.

'There was explosive dye in the cash machine,' Agnes explained to the two armed women, as Flash yelped and hit the deck. 'One of you check outside. It might be Forest Rangers. Some kind of ambush!'

As one woman sprinted towards the battered side door, Agnes kicked Flash hard in the stomach.

'Keep still, Peppa Pig!' she taunted. 'Unless you want another 10,000 volts.'

The woman who closed in on Robin looked strong and wore full army gear.

'The cash is ruined,' she shouted over the alarm. 'But Gisborne will still give us a hundred thousand for the brat.'

'We could ask for more,' Agnes suggested. 'That old fart's loaded and he wants Robin bad.'

Robin was still deaf in one ear, but the water from the overhead sprinkler had mostly flushed his blurry eye. His mind had cleared after the shock from the dye blast and he tried to control his panicked breathing and assess the situation:

Agnes only had a stun gun and was dealing with Flash.

One of the armed women was checking outside.

So only one gun posed an immediate threat.

'We need to tie these boys and throw 'em on the back of the pickup,' Agnes shouted. 'Where's the bag with the cuffs?'

Robin's bow and backpack were a few metres out of reach, but as his gun-toting opponent closed in, Robin slipped a hand into his trouser pocket and opened the blade of his pocket knife.

18. AIN'T THAT A KICK IN THE HEAD

The woman whose boot splattered into sprinkler water and sticky pink dye a few centimetres from Robin's face was a beefy thirty-something called Juno.

She'd read about Robin Hood. How he'd shot an arrow into gangster Guy Gisborne's dangly bits, robbed £100,000 from cash machines, flipped a cop car with a single arrow and become a figurehead for the growing resistance against police corruption and Sheriff Marjorie.

But in stressful situations our brains revert to stereotypes, and in this moment all Juno saw was a boy on the small side for his age, shivering pitifully from clothes soaked in cold water and pink gunge. She swung the rifle around to her back and gave Robin no consideration as she stared into the ATM.

'Looks like exploded bubble gum,' she shouted back to Agnes over the alarm.

'Just grab Robin,' Agnes shouted. 'Can't see Rangers or any ambush outside, but better not stick around to find out.'

Juno turned back and looked at Robin. 'On your feet, snot sack!'

Robin made a low groan and acted like he was too weak. Juno was getting drenched by the sprinkler, so she reached down hastily, grabbing a handful of Robin's shirt to drag him. As her first tug rolled Robin to one side, he whipped the knife out of his pocket and thrust it through the back of her right hand.

Juno stumbled back, almost slipping as she crashed into the side of the photo booth. Robin hoped Flash would join the fightback, but Agnes zapped him again the instant he moved.

'I'll wring your neck!' Juno roared.

At close range and with a knife sticking out of one hand, Juno went for Robin rather than the gun. Dye and water made the floor slippery, but Robin kept low and went under her arms. Without breaking stride, he snatched his bow and backpack, lobbed them over the Mario's Melts sandwich counter and made a gymnastic head-first dive after them.

He hadn't anticipated the fridge being so close behind the counter, and his head whacked it with a hollow thud before his elbow painfully bashed the floor. The tight counter space was a tangle, with his bow and backpack, plus bags and gear belonging to the two women who'd been waiting in ambush.

With his head throbbing, Robin shoved things out of the way to make space, then grabbed his bow. He rapidly slotted an arrow and hooked three more between the fingers of his left hand.

As Robin bobbed up, Juno was closing on the counter. She had the gun, but couldn't clench the fingers of her injured hand to hold it steady. From less than two metres Robin could hit anywhere he liked. But he was keen to injure rather than kill, so he shot an arrow through her left wrist to disable her other hand.

In the same instant, Flash figured that Agnes's stun gun took several seconds to recharge and made a grab while he was safe. Agnes caught him in the face with a powerful knee, but he managed to wrestle her down and snatch the zapper.

The third woman had returned from checking outside the building. She aimed her rifle when she saw Flash and Agnes battling, but Robin shot his bow first. She moved faster than Robin anticipated, so his arrow glanced her shoulder and became harmlessly trapped in the hood of her thick camouflage jacket.

But the near hit was enough of a distraction for Flash to grab the dangerous end of her gun. She squeezed off two shots. The bangs gave everyone a jolt, but the bullets went harmlessly over Flash's shoulder, trashing displays of AA batteries and vape juice.

Flash was strong, but a determined Agnes had locked one arm around his chunky legs and made a grab for the stun gun. After two rounds the rifle muzzle was hot, blistering the skin on Flash's palm as he tore the weapon away from its owner.

Robin realised Flash couldn't fight the two women simultaneously. He glanced around, satisfying himself that Juno wasn't in a fit state to shoot, then leaned over the counter and aimed at the woman in the doorway. As Flash kicked back at Agnes, knocking her away, Robin's arrow speared the other woman in the thigh.

Flash couldn't hold the hot metal, so the rifle clattered to the ground and he found the trigger on the stun gun and got Agnes back for zapping him.

Robin slotted another arrow, but his target backed out of the doorway and began a limping run outside, towards the battered Subaru.

'Dirty liar!' Flash roared, as he grabbed Agnes by the scruff of her blouse. His nose was badly broken where she'd kneed him and blood dribbled as he spoke. 'I ought to kill you. You told me you were done with SWU.'

'That's your weakness,' Agnes snarled back. 'You assume every girl loves you, but we really think you're an arse.'

Robin slid out from behind the sandwich counter. He kicked the rifle away from Juno as the deafening alarm coming out of the cash machine mercifully gave up. She was close to fainting from shock and it was uncomfortable looking at her bloody right hand and the arrow speared between the radius and ulna in her lower arm.

But Robin's sympathy was limited by the fact she'd come here with a plan to let him rob the cash machine, then take the proceeds and claim the bounty on his head.

'What now?' Flash asked Robin as he picked up the rifle. 'After I kill this one, obviously.'

'You're a joke,' Agnes snarled. 'You don't have the balls.'

'We're not killing anyone,' Robin told Flash firmly. 'They brought handcuffs for us. So, I guess we use 'em on these two and leave 'em to the Rangers. Then we get on the bikes, ride a few clicks and disappear into the trees.'

But out front the last woman standing had other ideas. It was painful driving with one leg numbed from the arrow sticking out of her thigh, but she managed. After accelerating towards the road, she turned back beneath the fuel-station canopy, driving a slow oval until the two dirt bikes were lined up between her headlamps.

She floored the gas, smashing the bikes with a front bull-bar. They spun and scraped. Chunks of plastic clattered into the Subaru's windscreen and caught under the front wheels. After backing up from the wreckage, she floored the accelerator again, heading north onto Old Road.

19. BOYS BASHED UP

'This ear's throbbing,' Robin complained, as Flash put a cuff on Agnes's wrist and locked the other end to the post on a shelving unit. 'Can't hear and my balance is off.'

'Too tight,' Agnes yelped.

'Good,' Flash told Agnes bitterly. 'I hope you enjoy prison.'

She gave Flash the finger with her free hand as he set off to cuff Juno. Since Juno's arms were both bloody, he cuffed her ankle to the stool in the photo booth.

Robin found a rotating sunglasses stand and studied his face in its little mirror. His hair was all gluey pink spikes, but what worried him was that his left ear was completely clogged with the stuff. He couldn't do much about his trousers, but he quickly swapped his soggy shirt for a souvenir hoodie with a picture of a waterfall and *Sensational Sherwood Forest* written on the back.

Flash's busted nose made his voice nasal. Strips of skin dangled from the palm he'd burned on the gun, but adrenaline rushing through his system overrode the pain.

'Get your stuff quickly,' Flash urged. 'Gonna be a long walk home.'

The sprinkler had stopped. Luckily Robin's bow and backpack had been out of range and he wasn't bothered about the cables and tools, but he was gutted to see his laptop in a puddle. Water drained from the ports when he picked it up, and there was liquid trapped under the screen that made rainbows when he touched it.

'Everything's on here,' Robin said, sounding wrecked. 'Passwords, hacking tools, pictures of my mum . . .'

'Back-ups?' Flash asked.

Robin shrugged. 'Some of it. I can probably get the data off if the hard drive is OK.'

'It's not our biggest problem right now,' Flash said. 'Rangers will be heading this way.'

Robin put the laptop in his backpack, picked up his bow and arrows and grabbed chocolate bars and bottles of water as they headed to the door.

'Rot in hell!' Agnes shouted, yanking her cuffs as Flash led the way out.

It felt colder. Mostly because Robin's trousers were soaked and his boots squelched with every step. Flash kept the assault rifle handy, but there were no women, no bandits attracted by the sound of shots and no Forest Rangers either.

There was a loud buzzing, and as they stepped out from the garage canopy a chunky orange drone with a camera under its belly swooped down, hovering three metres above their heads.

Flash swung around with the gun and took a couple of wild shots.

'It's just a camera,' Robin said. 'It can't follow us once we're in the trees.'

'You'd be surprised,' Flash said. 'Some of the little suckers have night vision and heat sensors.'

He led the way around the back of the service station. After jogging up a path signposted **Scenic View**, they reached a low fence and began scrambling down a steep embankment.

'Watch out for snakes,' Flash warned, as loose rocks broke under their boots.

It was too dark to see the drone, but even with his one good ear, Robin could hear that it was somewhere overhead as they sploshed through a stream at the bottom of the embankment and scrambled on through heavy undergrowth.

'You said Agnes was SWU,' Robin asked as they jogged. 'That's Sherwood Women's Union, right?'

'Right,' Flash agreed.

'They're the ones who got burned out by Castle Guards,' Robin said.

Flash nodded. 'Agnes has the scars to prove it.'

'But Will gave me the impression the SWU were OK.'

'They started up as a direct-action feminist group,' Flash explained. 'The name makes a lot of people think they're harmless. But over the years they dropped politics and turned into straight-up gangstas. Robbing, drug distribution, taking hostages.'

'How could you trust Agnes if you *knew* she was part of that?'

Flash sounded angry and defensive. '*Everyone* thought SWU was finished after their camp got incinerated. They always bought fuel and ammunition from the Brigands, so I've known Agnes since we were kids. She messaged while she was in hospital recovering from her burns. Told me she'd got a legit job and moved back with her parents.'

'Well, now we're screwed,' Robin said bitterly. 'Even if we get back to the mall, I am in so much trouble.'

'Look on the bright side,' Flash said, as they reached open ground around some abandoned farm buildings. 'Indio and Will are much nicer than the people I'm in trouble with.'

'I can still hear the drone,' Robin said, after they'd walked a little further. 'Guess you were right about heat sensors.'

'Makes a change for me to be right about something,' Flash sulked.

Robin stopped walking and reached for his bow.

'You walk out in the open,' Robin said. 'Not fast, but not so slow it looks suspicious.'

'It's dark – you'll never hit it.'

'I'm all ears if you've got a better idea,' Robin said, as he took a shooting position braced against a log.

Flash walked into the open, using a fake limp as an excuse to take it slow. Annoyingly the drone stayed back above the treeline. So, while Flash walked towards the barn, Robin darted through a copse of trees at the side to get a shooting angle.

When the drone's legs caught a scrap of moonlight it was almost directly over Robin's head. There were branches in the way and his balance was off with his blocked ear, but he fired three quick arrows.

The first hit leaves, the second clipped the drone, but not before Robin had released a third arrow that bounced off God knows what and almost speared him as it came back down. He deflected the arrow with his bow, while at the same time the drone crashed through branches and thudded onto soft ground less than ten metres away.

'Nice shooting!' Flash said, as he ran back into cover.

The pair scrambled on to where the drone had crashed and Robin took pleasure finding the body planted sideways in a puddle. He reached in, ripping off the camera and hurling it away.

'One problem solved,' Flash said, managing half a smile as he thumped Robin on the back with his unburned hand.

'Only about a million left,' Robin replied.

SPECIAL REPORT

'Good morning, this is Channel Fourteen serving the Central Region. I'm Kewpie Uzzle with your 6 a.m. headlines.

'Our lead story comes from the Seven Stars Service Station, situated on Old Road in the heart of Sherwood Forest. A little under two hours ago, it is believed Robin Hood and several unknown accomplices attempted to break into a cash machine, but the attempt was foiled by a sticky pink surprise! Our satellite van just arrived, and we're going to take you straight across to Susan at the crime scene.'

The picture cut from the studio to a moody shot of an arrow surrounded by drips of blood. The camera operator panned sideways to show the busted cash machine and the pink mess around it, then stopped on Susan the reporter, who held a microphone with a bright yellow bulb, a Channel Fourteen logo around its handle.

'Thanks, Kewpie,' Susan began dramatically. 'I arrived on the scene ten minutes ago and found Forest Rangers and a forensic team bagging evidence. Nobody is completely clear what happened, but I can tell you that this badly botched raid led to all kinds of chaos.

'As I look around this gas-station shop, I can see blood, arrows, several bullet holes and lots of this exploded neon dye. Forest Rangers are not issuing any statement at this stage, but with me now is the only known eyewitness, Agnes McIntyre. Agnes, you've had quite a night, so we appreciate you talking to us at this difficult time.'

The camera operator zoomed out gently to show Agnes with pink splats on her Seven Stars uniform. The harsh on-camera light caught a sweaty brow and cuffs hanging off one wrist.

'Agnes, what happened?'

'I'd just started my 3 a.m. shift,' Agnes began, before sniffling. 'I heard bikes and a Subaru truck. I figured they were stopping for fuel, but there was a big crash as someone kicked in the side door.

'The company trains us to do whatever robbers say if there's a raid, but there was this one guy they were calling Flash. He was *really* creepy and he punched me and threatened to hurt me, even though all I did was kneel down and let them handcuff me to that shelving unit over there.'

'How many robbers were there?' Susan asked.

'Four, maybe five,' Agnes lied. 'At first they were calm. I recognised Robin Hood because he had a bow and arrow. He opened the cash machine and it was all calm.

'But when that dye exploded, his gang started fighting and arguing. I was scared because a gun went off. And one of the women tried to say something to Robin, but he went berserk and shot her for no reason. That's why there's drips of blood everywhere.'

'And then they left?'

Agnes nodded. 'They kept arguing. One of them drove the truck into the bikes they had parked outside, smashing them up. I was left on my own, still handcuffed to the shelf unit. After they left, I managed to lift the metal shelves off, so I could pull the cuffs over the top and set myself free.'

'And you're still wearing the cuffs?'

Agnes held her wrist up to show the camera. 'The Forest Rangers gave me a hot drink and blanket to calm my nerves, and there's a locksmith on the way to cut these off.'

'Finally, do you have any message for Robin Hood and the other robbers?' Susan asked.

'I am a *totally* peaceful person,' Agnes said, cracking a wholesome smile. 'I've been working here part-time, saving money for when I start university in September. I know there are a lot of problems around Sherwood, but robbing only makes that worse.'

'Powerful words,' Susan said, as she gave the camera a solemn look. 'And now back to Kewpie in the studio.'

20. WHERE ARE YOU, BUTTFACE?

Marion was steaming at Robin, but even more furious that nobody believed a word she said. It was now eight in the morning and she'd already been through everything once with her mum Indio. Now Azeem had come down from the roof with a message that Will Scarlock wanted to speak to Marion in the command tent.

'It's better to be honest,' Indio told Marion gently as they followed Azeem up wooden steps to the roof.

Inside the tent, Will was dressed in a tank top and pyjama bottoms, while two screens that normally displayed security footage had been switched to Channel Fourteen and News 24.

News 24 had a reporter standing outside Seven Stars Service Station. Marion noticed three satellite vans and more reporters and camera operators in the background, along with half a dozen orange Forest Ranger trucks. The scrolling news ticker beneath said: **POLICE HUNT FOR ROBIN HOOD — SUSPECTS COVERED IN PINK DYE.**

'This has made an interesting start to my day,' Will said, drinking coffee from a *Stop Climate Change* mug as he faced Marion and Indio across the big planning table. 'So, Marion, tell us what you know.'

'You're not in trouble, sweetie,' Indio added. 'But it's vital we find Robin and Flash before the Forest Rangers do.'

'Mum, I'm not lying!' Marion growled. 'For the *fifth* time!'

'Let's stay calm,' Will said soothingly. 'Tell us what happened.'

Marion rolled her eyes. 'I woke up about quarter to six. I was thirsty, so I went to find my water bottle. When I walked past Robin's bed he wasn't there. I figured he'd gone to pee in the bucket outside, because sometimes the squeaky door hinges wake me up.

'Then I noticed his stuff was gone. Boots, phone, bow. I wasn't worried. Karma and Finn are often up early, so I thought he'd probably gone down to have breakfast with them. But when I checked outside, the motion sensor at the top of the escalator hadn't been switched off. And I was, like, *That's weird*.

'So I turned it off and walked down. As I got there two security blokes were arriving, looking for Robin because they'd seen the story on Channel Fourteen and didn't believe it.'

Will placed his elbows on the table and gave Marion a serious stare. 'I'm not saying I don't believe you, but I *don't* understand how Robin could have left the sports store without someone turning off the motion sensors and turning them back on after.'

'You and Robin are tight,' Azeem added. 'This must have taken a lot of planning.'

Marion thumped furiously on the table. 'I know none of you believe me. You say he can't have got out without my help. All I can say is, it's Robin Hood. He climbs like a cat, he hacks computers, and here . . .'

Marion dramatically unlocked her phone and looked upset as she slid it across the table.

'Look at all my emails, my messages to Robin. There's no conspiracy, right up to this morning when I texted him: **Where are you buttface?**

'The only thing I know is, Flash came to him about a week ago with some idea. I told Robin not to get involved. I love my big brother, but he's no genius.'

Will nodded slowly. He'd known Marion since she was a toddler, and thought she was an honest person.

'I believe you,' he said.

Marion scowled back at her mum. 'Glad *someone* does.'

Indio put her arm on Marion's back, but she batted it off and spoke to Will. 'Do you think we'll find them?'

'Sherwood is immense,' Will said. 'We don't have manpower for a search, but neither do the Forest Rangers.'

As he finished saying this, his walkie-talkie blasted to life.

'This is the watchtower. We have eyeballs on two males approaching via the south parking lot. I think it's our boys.'

Will pulled the radio hooked on the waistband of his pyjamas. 'Are you sure, Neil?'

A laugh crackled down the radio. 'They're extremely pink!'

21. HURL YA GUTS

As Marion followed Azeem and Will down from the rooftop tent, she imagined two versions of seeing Robin in her head.

In the first, she grabbed him and yelled, calling him an irresponsible little twerp and reminding him that she'd warned him not to get involved with Flash.

In the second version she just walked up and boxed him on the nose.

But when Marion saw the two failed robbers stumble into Designer Outlets from the disused southern end of the mall, her rage was replaced by pity. Flash looked exhausted and his nose was a bloody mess. Robin could barely walk and the bits of his skin that weren't neon pink were ghost white.

'Robin keeps puking,' Flash told Will. 'Says his head hurts and he can hardly walk in a straight line.'

Will was more interested in speaking to the guard who'd let them in, getting the watchtower to confirm that the boys hadn't been tailed by Forest Rangers, or worse.

'You both need Dr Gladys,' Azeem said, then grabbed Robin around the waist and threw him easily over her shoulder. 'Marion, grab Robin's gear.'

Marion grunted as she grabbed the stuff, which included two heavy assault rifles taken from the SWU.

'I want a guard on these two until they've been questioned,' Will told his radio, as he caught up.

Other mall residents saw Flash and Robin and gave chase. They'd seen the news reports and fired questions about what had happened.

'Why did you slap that nice girl Agnes around?' an elderly woman asked Flash furiously.

'Just a teenager saving for university. You should be ashamed of yourself!' another disgusted voice added.

Flash looked baffled.

'Let's get them out of sight,' Will said anxiously, as they neared the clinic.

The clinic was built in the remains of a high-end clothing store. Government hospitals weren't allowed to treat refugees or anyone without identity documents, so it was the only medical facility available for thousands of Forest People. It ran on donations, with three nurses and a single elderly doctor, who was tiny, blunt and close to celebrating her eighty-fourth birthday.

Azeem kicked the door of a waiting area crammed with twenty non-urgent patients, many of them kids who all seemed to be screaming. As Flash staggered in behind, they went through another swinging door into a triage area.

'Are there any beds?' Azeem shouted as she glanced around. There were a dozen patients bedded in a small ward off to one side, and four more occupied beds lined against the walls of an area that was supposed to be used for examinations.

'He'll have to go on the examination table,' a nurse said, as he rushed by holding a drip bag.

Azeem carried Robin through to a side room, where a couple of elderly patients sat in chairs. She laid him on two tables pushed together with a yoga mat on top.

'I feel sick again,' Robin moaned.

'Make way!' Dr Gladys shouted, pushing past Will, Marion and Azeem. 'Why are you all back here? I'm running a clinic, not a blasted circus!'

She turned to Robin. 'Feel sick?' she asked.

'Yeah,' Robin croaked. 'But my stomach's empty, so I just retch. And my head is throbbing so bad.'

The doctor showed zero sympathy. 'That's what you get for running off doing daft things and worrying everyone silly!'

She rocked Robin's head side to side, squinted as she shone a light into his left ear, then experimentally scratched at the pink stuff crusted to his skin.

'How's your balance?'

'Wobbly,' Robin answered.

'Your inner ear contains cells called otoconia that control balance,' the doctor explained. 'When your ear gets blocked or infected, they stop working. We'll get a nurse to scoop out as much pink stuff as we can, then flush the rest with a syringe.'

'Is that painful?' Robin asked.

'Not as painful as what you deserve,' Dr Gladys said, before stepping outside and giving Flash an even briefer examination. 'Broken nose! Buy painkillers from the pharmacy and make an appointment to have it reset if you don't like how it looks when the swelling goes down.'

22. THRILL-SEEKING PERSONALITY

With only two nurses on duty and a ton of patients with problems more serious than a clogged ear, Robin had to wait five queasy hours before a nurse had time to sort him out. When he was finally free to go, his head throbbed, his feet were horribly blistered from walking in wet boots and he had a giant swelling where his elbow thumped the floor behind the sandwich counter.

But the pain wasn't as bad as Robin's sense of shame. He needed a towel and clean clothes before he could take a shower. He tried sneaking into the sports store and up to his den without being spotted, but Otto was charging around, pulling Finn in a wooden cart, and Karma was keeping an eye on them.

'Marion says she's not talking to you,' Karma told Robin. 'I downloaded a product safety sheet from a company that makes dye packs. It says the pink will dissolve with a mixture of washing-up liquid and lemon juice. I mixed a batch and put it up by your bed in the clear bottle, with a couple of scouring pads.'

'Thanks,' Robin said. 'Is Flash around?'

'There was a rumour that some Brigands have snuck into the mall to sort him out,' Karma explained. 'I think he cleaned up, then went into hiding.'

After getting his stuff, Robin headed up to the roof and took the longest shower of his life. Scraping the pink stuff off his skin wasn't too bad, though the wiry pads and strong detergent left his skin raw. Hair was the nightmare, because the dye had dried in clumps like marshmallow that had to be picked out, and Karma's cleaning mix contained lemon juice, which he knew all about when a tiny bit got in his eye.

After a zombielike walk back to his den, Robin saw that Marion had taken her bedding and the rest of her stuff back downstairs. He'd missed a whole night's sleep, but his mind kept going when he lay on his bed, so he moved to the sofa and felt sorry for himself as he flicked on the aged TV for the early-evening news.

The good thing was that two viewers who'd seen Agnes in earlier bulletins remembered her from a Sherwood Women's Union kidnapping and called Channel Fourteen to say she wasn't the innocent gas-station attendant she'd claimed to be in her TV interview.

The bad was that Agnes heard she'd been rumbled before the Forest Rangers. She'd knocked out a radio journalist while he was taking a leak and escaped in his car.

As Robin watched he used the last drops of Karma's cleaning solution to clean his bow, then found a small screwdriver and used it to disassemble his busted laptop. The inside was full of trapped pinkish water and it was clearly beyond repair.

But Robin knew the metal platters that hold data inside hard-disk drives have an airtight seal, so his hacking tools, passwords and family photos ought to be retrievable. He used his phone to search for *water-damaged hard drive*.

According to YouTube tutorials, the best technique was to seal the damaged hard drive in an airtight box filled with grains of uncooked rice. After a day, the rice would have absorbed all the moisture from the circuits and you could recover your data. Both videos warned about the dangers of powering up the drive too soon, because a single drip of water could be enough to cause a short-circuit and kill the unit.

Robin undid more screws, pulled a plug and retrieved the playing-card-sized hard drive. As he dried the worst of the moisture on an old T-shirt, he figured he'd be able to get a plastic box and some rice if he went to the Maid family den downstairs. But they'd probably be having dinner and he dreaded facing everyone. Especially Marion.

He'd spent ten minutes working up the nerve to go downstairs when he heard boots on the escalator.

'Can I come in?' Will Scarlock asked.

'Free country,' Robin said warily.

In addition to noticing Will's horrendous brown teeth, Robin spotted that he was holding a screw-top bottle filled with a creamy orange liquid and a zip-up pouch under one arm.

Robin shuffled over so Will could join him on the sofa.

'Mango lassi,' Will said as he passed Robin the bottle. 'Indio said it's one of your favourites. And there's curry and rice downstairs if you're hungry.'

Robin was thirsty and took two gulps of the sweet yoghurt drink.

'I'm really sorry I caused everyone trouble,' he said weakly, as he wiped a creamy moustache with his little finger.

'I've got five kids, including four lads,' Will said warmly. 'Neo's the youngest and he's grown up now. I like to think I know a bit about raising boys, but my four all made big mistakes along the way.'

'As bad as me?' Robin asked.

'Sam was the wildest,' Will admitted. 'Though he didn't make it to the TV news. My point is, experience has taught me that yelling and punishing your kids doesn't do much. The important thing is to work out why a mistake happened and make sure everyone learns from it.

'Robin, I'm not a psychologist, but I think you have what they call a *thrill-seeking personality*. You're clever, you're independent, but you get bored easily and you *love* taking risks, whether it's dropping a skateboard off a crazy ramp, or robbing a cash machine. Do you know the worst thing you can do to a thrill seeker?'

He paused, but Robin didn't know the answer and kept staring into his lassi.

'You're like a big ball of energy,' Will said. 'When Gisborne put that fat bounty on your head, Indio and I saw the danger you were in and did everything we could to keep you safe. But by not letting you have any independence, we made you so crazy that . . .'

Robin finished Will's sentence. 'I ran off and did something super-dumb.'

Will laughed and slapped Robin on the back. 'I'm not saying you're not responsible for what happened. But it's our fault too, because we didn't listen to your needs.'

'Does this mean I'm not getting punished?' Robin asked hopefully.

'In your dreams, pal!' Will said, clapping his hands and switching to a harsher tone. 'You can catch up on sleep tomorrow, but for a month after that you're gonna be up at six every morning, feeding chickens, collecting eggs and cleaning crap out of their sheds.'

'I deserve it,' Robin admitted.

'But I've spoken with Karma and Indio. We're going to let you be more involved in things and try to help you make better decisions. I'll probably never be able to give you as much freedom as you want, because you're a crazy twelve-year-old with a bounty on your head. But I promise we'll listen and try to stop you dying of boredom.'

As Robin nodded, Will held out the pouch he'd brought in under his arm.

'I got what you asked for,' he said. 'Details of Sherwood Castle's IT systems, from my source.'

'That was quick,' Robin said, as he pointed awkwardly towards the damp computer parts. 'But I'll need a new laptop. There's only so much you can do with a phone.'

'Your share from the Captain Cash job is upstairs in the safe,' Will said, as he stood up from the little sofa. 'Let me know how much you need, and don't be scared to go downstairs and grab some food. You're not Indio and Karma's favourite person right now, but you've got to eat.'

'Is Marion down there?' Robin asked.

'She is, and I suggest you be careful,' Will said, cracking a big smile as he headed out of Robin's den. 'Marion has her father's temper and she said something about *kicking the little twerp's butt.*

PART III
NEARLY THREE WEEKS LATER

23. DEAD POSH SCHOOL RUN

The Jackson Pollock splatter painting in the white stone hallway of Sheriff Marjorie's penthouse was worth fifty times more than the entire crumbling Hood homestead where Little John had lived for the first sixteen years of his life.

His mother's wealth also bought a robot dog, a thirty-seat home cinema, balconies with spectacular views over Sherwood's green canopy, twenty-four-hour room service and access to the resort's pool, spa and gym.

But while John's material needs had been met in the three weeks since he'd left Locksley High, the penthouse often felt like a lavish prison. His mother was always on the go, with Sheriff duties and King Corporation business, while the castle's location in the forest made it hard to visit pals back in Locksley.

John also felt an emotional hole, left by loss of contact with his gentle but eccentric father. He even missed Robin, though the brothers had battled through childhood, teasing each other and playing every prank, from harmless apple-pie beds to the time Robin put ink in John's shampoo bottle.

It was early on a Monday morning and John was due to start his new school in under two hours. He'd towelled off after a shower and stood at the full-length mirror in his bedroom, fearing that his new schoolmates would instantly decide he was a freak.

He'd been swimming and working out every day, but being able to order any food he wanted from a phone beside his bed cancelled out most of the benefits. He thought his arms and shoulders looked better from lifting weights, but he hated his fat thighs and wobbly belly.

John thought about making himself look more buff by putting on one of the tight compression shirts he wore for rugby, but it would be too hot under his new school's striped blazer and matching tie.

John crunched a half-rasher of bacon left on his breakfast tray and looked at the uniform laid out on the bed. All his clothes went into the five-star resort's laundry, coming back immaculately ironed and wrapped in an environmentalist's nightmare of disposable hangers, cellophane wrap and tissue paper. Even his gym socks went in a laundry press, before being tied with red ribbon and scented with a spritz of sandalwood.

His new school's largest standard uniform wasn't close to fitting, so one had been handstitched by a Nottingham tailor and Little John liked the way it looked, fitting like uniforms rarely do on the first day of school.

'Not bad!' John told himself, as he buttoned the blazer and dabbed gel to tame his hair.

New shoes scraped the back of his heel as he stepped out of his bedroom. He hoped to find his mum out on the balcony where she liked to take breakfast. But Sheriff Marjorie's enormous bedroom had its double doors open, with a breeze billowing curtains as a maid in canary-yellow uniform stripped sheets off the bed.

'Pia, have you seen my mum?' John asked.

She shook her head. 'Sheriff left already. You look so smart!'

'Thanks,' John said, but wished someone closer than a maid was around to offer support on his first day.

John was going to be a flexi-boarder, staying at school during the week but coming home most weekends. He grabbed his backpack and wheelie case and took a last glance back at damp footprints and rumpled sheets that would be cleaned up long before he returned.

It was a mark of how John's life had changed that it no longer felt special stepping onto Sherwood Castle's rooftop helipad and ducking as he strode beneath whipping blades of a silver chopper with black King Corporation logo on the tail.

As the pilot gave him a nod, John had his pick of seven quilted leather recliners. A ground marshal secured John's luggage with a strap, and they were airborne seconds after the passenger door thudded shut.

The rising sun made Sherwood look spectacular. Deep green stretched away from the castle in every direction, broken only by the pollution haze rising off Route 24. John reached forward and grabbed a can of iced coffee from a little fridge, then worried as he imagined Robin as a tiny speck somewhere down in the forest.

Barnsdale School was a couple of kilometres from Sherwood's northern border. Two and a half hours from Sherwood Castle by road, but thirty minutes in the chopper.

John worried he'd be making a scene arriving by helicopter, but as they approached over the school's two-kilometre rowing lake and coiffured playing fields, he eyed four helipads, with a small chopper lifting off and two more spilling uniformed kids on the ground.

John wasn't sure where to walk as he opened the door to step out, but a handsome man in a brown suit jogged over and shook his hand.

'John Kovacevic?' the man asked. 'I'm Mr Zhang, your assigned mentor.'

John cringed at his mother's surname. Sheriff Marjorie said it was better to drop *Hood* because of Ardagh and Robin's notoriety. She'd made the decision and had her assistant fill out the school paperwork without bothering to consult her son.

As his wheelie case click-clacked on a paved path leading to a grand nineteenth-century school building, kids who knew where they were going ran past with backpacks.

'It's unusual for us to take a pupil with only half a term before summer break,' Mr Zhang explained. 'But it will give you a chance to make friends and settle before you start International Baccalaureate studies in September.'

John nodded. 'That's what my mum said, though maybe she just wants me out of the house!'

Mr Zhang halted to scold a little kid who bolted off the lawn and swerved in front of them. After another minute they'd walked up six steps and into the school's main lobby.

Varnished wood, vaulted ceilings and spiral stairs leading up to a clock tower made a grander impression than Locksley High, though the aroma made John realise that rich and poor teens give off exactly the same stink.

'There's one other pupil joining our school today,' Mr Zhang said, as he pointed towards a battered wooden door off to one side. 'I'll give you both a tour of our facilities, then take you to your dorm rooms to unpack. If you'd be kind enough to wait in reception, I just need to grab your timetables from the admin office.'

'No problem, sir,' John said, as he turned the brass doorknob and wheeled his case into a reception room, with an unlit marble fireplace and old leather sofas.

Little John's jaw dropped as he saw the other new arrival staring out of a window at the school grounds.

'I saw you walk up the steps,' Clare Gisborne said, as she turned and glared. 'Bit of a shocker, eh?'

24. MEANWHILE AT DESIGNER OUTLETS

'Robin!' Karma said, her voice stiff as she rocked him awake.

Robin woke with a start. He saw Karma's belly, which now looked very pregnant. He also saw his bed covered with notepads and computer printouts and his swanky new gaming laptop, which was the most awesome thing he'd ever owned.

'What time is it?' Robin asked, cracking a yawn.

'Eight thirty!'

He sat up sharply and was planning to say something like, *Oh God, I slept through my alarm*, when he realised there was an object stuck to his cheek. There were rats and mice inside the mall, so that was his first thought as he panicked and whacked it away.

But as Karma cracked up laughing, Robin felt sticky stuff on his cheek, sniffed chocolate on his fingertips and then saw the Snickers bar he'd batted away, and melted chocolate smeared over his pillow.

'That'll teach you to eat in bed,' Karma said, laughing so hard she had to pull one of the chairs out from the little dining table and sit down. 'I wish I'd videoed that!'

Robin saw the funny side as he scrambled out of bed. There was no tap in his den, so he poured water from a big drinking bottle onto a dirty T-shirt and used it to rub chocolate off his face.

'I got a message on one of my hacking forums,' Robin explained, as he wiped. 'Tons of info about StayNet security breaches and back doors.'

Karma looked confused. 'StayNet?'

Robin sounded excited as he explained. 'Will's source found out that Sherwood Castle uses a suite of hospitality applications called StayNet. The software handles *everything*, with modules for reservations, room service, staff rotas, even the casino.'

'The Sheriff's a dark horse,' Karma said. 'It would be huge if we could see some of what her people are up to.'

'I got a pirated copy of StayNet running on my laptop, and posted on a hacking forum to ask if anyone had ever hacked a StayNet system,' Robin explained. 'I got a detailed reply as I was getting in bed last night, and the info was *gold*. I started reading through all the stuff she sent, making notes. I must have dozed off, cos I've been getting up at five forty to go deal with the chickens.'

He stepped closer to Karma and showed her his cheek. 'Did I get all the chocolate?'

Karma grabbed the damp T-shirt and wiped brown smears from Robin's chin and earlobe. As he hurriedly pulled on tracksuit bottoms and boots, she stripped his pillowcase and bedsheet.

'I can do that later,' Robin said.

'You really *will* have mice in your bed if you leave mashed up Snickers everywhere.'

'Chicken Sheila is gonna have a right go at me,' Robin complained, as he pocketed his phone. 'She's grumpy enough when I arrive on time.'

'Sheila's harmless,' Karma said.

'Could you text her? Say I'm sick or something.'

Karma held out a balled-up bedsheet covered with brown chocolate stains. 'How about we take a photo of this and tell her you've got diarrhoea?'

Robin laughed, but Karma turned more serious. 'You're not getting off. You stayed up until stupid o'clock and slept through your alarm. Your fault, your consequences.'

'Whatever,' Robin sighed, as he headed out.

As he slid down the rubber handrail of the escalator, Robin realised one of his boot laces was undone, but instead of stopping to tie it, he hurdled Finn's pushbike, shot into the Maid family den and grabbed two apples from a bowl for his breakfast as he wished Indio and Matt good morning.

Then he almost bumped into Marion. She wore a Nottingham Kangaroos cap and a set of overalls splattered in grey roof resin.

'Sorry,' Robin blurted.

But Marion still wasn't talking to him, so she tutted and shook her head.

25. STUCK IN THE MIDDLE WITH YOU

Little John imagined Clare Gisborne charging at him. He eyed the metal poker by the fireplace as a potential weapon, but it was first day at a new school and they were both on best behaviour.

Clare backed away from the window and sat on a sofa. John sat opposite, with a glass coffee table and a vase of half-dead flowers between them. He'd never seen Clare in a skirt before and her jiggling foot made her look as nervous as he felt.

'That idiot Zhang's taking his time,' Clare said, breaking the awkward silence.

'Yeah,' John agreed, then after a pause, 'I can't believe they kicked you out of Locksley High.'

Clare tutted. 'They didn't. But the Monday after I got soaked, someone spat on my jacket. Day after that there was rude graffiti about me all over the toilets. The last straw was my locker getting broken into. They found my books in a flooded sink in the chemistry lab.'

'Pretty nasty,' John said, but at the same time thought, *If anyone ever deserved that . . .*

'Like you care,' Clare grunted. 'It's the Hood family stirring trouble that started all this!'

'Sheriff Marjorie is my mum, Robin's my brother, Ardagh's my dad. I'm just a guy stuck in the middle of all the nonsense.'

'That's a problem we have in common,' Clare said, as she eyed the fancy gold-leaf ceiling. 'This place might be OK though. Locksley High is mostly held up by the mould and dirt, and most teachers are only there for the money.'

'Did you see that rowing lake as you flew in?' John asked. 'Must have spent millions dredging that out.'

'Came by car,' Clare said peevishly. 'We're not poor, but we don't live in castles and fly helicopters.'

John felt embarrassed. 'I'm supposed to be here on some rugby scholarship,' he said. 'But I watched videos of Barnsdale playing. Those dudes are *way* above my standard.'

'I'll sign up for soccer,' Clare said. 'Maybe showjumping if my dad stumps up the extra money.'

'Kids won't be scared to tackle you here.'

Clare grunted and John felt like he'd overstepped.

'Sorry,' John said. 'I just . . .'

Clare sat forward, looking thoughtful. 'This is a fresh start, right? What if we leave our beefs back in Locksley?

We'll probably be in a few of the same classes, but it shouldn't be hard to ignore each other.'

John could have pointed out that it was Clare and her flunkeys who'd strutted around Locksley High picking fights. But despite his sense of righteousness and the fact he trusted Clare like he'd trust a starving dog with a leg of roast lamb, John saw no downside in trying to live a peaceful existence.

'Happy to ignore you,' John agreed.

'Shake,' Clare said, gobbing generously in her palm before reaching across the table.

John hesitated. The spit was gross, and Clare's judo and kick-boxing skills meant she could probably turn the handshake into some sort of armlock and stick his head through the glass table.

'It's a deal,' John said, feeling spit squelch as they shook, and relief when Clare let go without doing him any damage.

26. ROOFTOP PRESSURE WASH

Chicken Sheila was all about chickens, from her frizzy black hair down to boots crusted in white bird manure. She grew up on a poultry farm, spent years raising award-winning birds in sheds near Locksley and when Guy Gisborne's thugs made her sell her land for a pittance to make way for a rubbish tip, Sheila hatched new flocks at Designer Outlets.

'Come on time or don't come at all!' she growled, when Robin approached the rooftop sheds. 'Leaving me to pick all the eggs, with my bad back and all!'

This was about what Robin expected.

'Is there something else I could do to make up the time?' he suggested reasonably. 'You mentioned some of the sheds need painting.'

'I ain't got paint yet!' she spat. 'I spoke to Scarlock already. Will says if you're no use here, to send you over to Unai – he always needs an extra hand fixing the roof.'

It took Robin ages to find Unai. He was repairing the seal around a skylight, while Marion was in the background using a jet washer to blast moss out of gutters.

'I asked Will for help, but never you!' Unai growled, as he wagged a finger in Robin's face. 'You worked with me one time and shot more holes in my roof than you fixed!'

Robin groaned and looked up at the sky. 'If everyone thinks I'm so incompetent, can I go back to bed?'

But Unai wasn't having that. As he lit a cigarette, he pointed to Marion.

'Fetch the water for her.'

Robin felt wary as he approached Marion. She'd not been up to his den or said anything more than, *Pass the butter*, or, *Get out of my way*, since he ran off with Flash.

Not talking to Marion was easy when he ate in the Maid family den, because it was always mayhem with Karma, Otto, Finn, Matt and usually a bunch of guests. But here it was just Marion, Robin and a huge grey roof.

'Why are you here?' Marion spat, lifting off plastic goggles and propping them in her hair.

'Unai told me to fetch water,' Robin explained, wary of the powerful sprayer in Marion's hand.

'Get on with it then,' she said bluntly, pointing to an empty plastic water tank behind the one connected to the sprayer.

There was no running water on, or anywhere near, this part of the roof, so Robin had to lift the tank onto Unai's trolley, wheel it several hundred metres across the roof to the shower block, fill it from a hose, then bring it back for Marion.

The sun had a kick, and with no shade Robin's clothes were soaked in sweat after two round trips. At the start of his third, Unai gave Robin money and told him to buy snacks from a rooftop cafe.

When Robin got back, Unai took his change, coffee and baguette and stepped away from the flammable putty he'd been using to have another smoke. Marion stripped thick rubber gloves and caught her breath as she sat with her legs swinging off a ventilation shaft.

'Jet washing goes quicker with you fetching the water,' she admitted as she peeled foil from her cheese-and-tomato toastie.

Robin sensed a friendlier tone and said the least controversial thing he could think of.

'How many hours do you have to work today?'

'Two like every other kid,' Marion explained. 'But Unai has heaps to do, so if I don't have a study session, I stick around till the job's done.'

'Nice of you,' Robin said, as he bit into a sausage roll.

'Unai's been teaching me roofing and carpentry skills,' Marion said. 'And Designer Outlets is a community. It ticks me off when people do the minimum, then buzz off and do their own thing.'

Robin wondered if that was a dig at him for running off with Flash. But he didn't act offended because he didn't want Marion going back to silent treatment.

'I meant it when I told everyone I was sorry,' Robin said, trying to sound pitiful.

Marion stood up like she was irritated. Robin thought he'd blown it, but she turned back.

'I'm still angry about a *lot* of things, Robin. You made a big fancy plan behind my back. You didn't listen when I told you not to get involved with Flash. And now Flash has run off and I'm worried sick because nobody knows where he is.'

Robin shrugged. 'Flash is years older than me. Shouldn't he be the responsible one?'

'You're brainy and always saying you hate being treated like a kid,' Marion snorted. 'So you can't blame a goofy idiot like Flash for leading you astray.'

'Fair,' Robin sighed as he opened a can of Rage Cola.

'Flash is probably having fun with some trashy forest woman,' Marion said. 'But you made my mums, brothers and a bunch of other people worry about you.'

Robin realised he'd get nowhere fighting Marion on details, so he switched to an emotional plea.

'I miss having you as a friend,' Robin said. 'And I don't like sleeping in the dark on my own.'

Marion smiled. 'It's *adorable* that you're still scared of the dark!'

He tutted. 'I hate it when you say I'm *adorable*.'

'I know,' Marion said. 'That's *why* I say it.'

After a pause, she added, 'I've missed hanging out with you. And I miss the upstairs den whenever Matt wakes up with a screaming nightmare, or Karma farts, or Finn crawls in my bed at 2 a.m. with freezing-cold feet.'

'Cut the yapping, lovebirds!' Unai shouted as he tapped on his wristwatch. 'Let's get this job done before it gets even hotter out here.'

Robin wiped pastry grease down his tracksuit bottoms and stepped towards an empty water tank.

'Give us a hand before you get the water,' Marion said. 'I changed the water jet before break and it's leaking. I think I cross-threaded the nozzle, but I can't see where when I'm at this end pulling the trigger.'

Robin looked at the sprayer lance as she turned the pressure down to minimum and drizzled some water.

'I don't think it's leaking,' Robin said.

'Not the side,' Marion said, tapping the sprayer. 'The little ball nozzle at the tip.'

'What little nozzle?' Robin asked as he looked around the end of the lance. 'I can't see anything.'

Marion dialled up the pressure before pulling the trigger. Robin gasped and coughed as he stumbled backwards.

She punched air and howled with laughter. 'I do not *believe* you fell for that!'

'Hell!' Robin hacked, spitting water and pushing wet hair out of his eyes, before laughing and shaking his head.

Marion cracked an evil smile as she snapped her goggles back down over her eyes. 'And now we're even.'

27. THEM SAME OLD QUESTIONS

After the shock of Clare, the rest of John's first day at Barnsdale School was an anticlimax. Lunch was edible. It was exam season, so he spent the afternoon in revision sessions he didn't need and for after-school activity he picked debate club.

The subject was: *Is the current government doing enough to fight poverty?*

John was assigned to a group researching for a debate the following week. His three female teammates all seemed super-posh, and hearing them talk about poverty felt like sumo wrestlers discussing the finer points of a ballet.

John was naturally shy, and he kept quiet until a girl called Leia got bored enough to back up her wheelchair and ask where he was from.

He told her his name was Kovacevic, but Leia saw right through it and squealed, 'OMG you're Robin Hood's brother!'

In an instant, John went from lonely-new-kid to superstar and all the girls were asking questions.

'Are you in touch with Robin?'

'Can you shoot a bow as well as your brother?'

'Where's Robin now?'

'How long can Robin hide from Gisborne?'

'Is it true Sheriff Marjorie has a secret prison in the Sherwood Castle basement?'

'Was your dad really framed by the cops?'

'Have you visited your dad on Pelican Island?'

'What will Robin do next?'

John's appeal diminished when they realised his answers were all *no* or *I don't know*, but he still had to fake grin his way through a bunch of selfies.

It wasn't the worst thing that could happen on your first day of school, but he still felt grumpy and awkward as he walked back to his little dorm room.

Teens chased up and down the hallways outside and there was a near-riot in the kitchen area, where pupils could make toast and hot drinks. John stayed in his room, putting books on the shelf over his desk and hanging clothes in the wardrobe.

'You're famous,' Clare Gisborne said, sounding friendly rather than menacing.

John spun and saw her standing in his doorway. Her shorts and Locksley Kangaroos shirt had grass stains and her socks were pushed down, exposing battered shin pads. John also noted a red welt under one eye and scabs forming on a bloody knee.

'So, I'm sitting on the toilet after football,' Clare explained. 'These girls come into the bathroom, and they're all like, *SQUEEEE! Did you hear that new Year Eleven kid is Robin Hood's brother? SQUEEEE! I want to kiss him and be the mother of his babies . . .*'

John gawped. 'They said that?'

Clare smiled. 'I made up the kissing and babies part, but they sounded so thrilled you might have a shot.'

John laughed, then stopped because it felt utterly weird having crazy-evil Clare Gisborne standing in his doorway making jokes.

'You look beat up,' John said.

Clare nodded, then told her battle story with relish. 'Coach let me start as striker and said, *Show me what you've got.* This beefy defender marking me kept giving verbals – saying my dad was scum and my accent was common.

'I bit my tongue, until she slid in with a leg-breaker tackle. Luckily I hurdled and just caught my sock on her stud. But after that it was game on! I sucker-punched her when the ref wasn't looking. Then she got booked for another tackle on me that should have been straight red. So I waited until just before final whistle and ran my studs down her leg. Turned into a monster scrap, almost every player. She punched me, I punched her. Four of us got sent off! Absolutely brilliant fun!'

'Did you win?' John asked.

Clare shrugged. 'I scored a great volley, but I forget the result . . . Do you mind if I come in?'

John felt uneasy but nodded, then breathed Clare's sweat as she pulled out the chair under his desk and sat with elbows on the backrest and her legs astride it.

'My dad's an arse!' she spat, then looked up at John with needy eyes.

He'd seen Clare get yelled at and bullied by her dad, but her admission felt huge.

'Parents are tricky,' John said.

'I called him at lunchtime,' Clare said. 'Told him it was weird being away from home and not knowing anyone, and he just grunted.

'Then I said I'd bumped into you. And suddenly he was super-excited. He starts ranting about how he's sure you're still in contact with Robin. And that I should make friends with you, and I should try and get on your laptop and read your emails.

'I swear, my dad cares more about catching your little brother than my happiness.'

'My mum's as bad,' John admitted. 'She changed my surname without asking. And whenever I ask about visiting my dad, she comes up with all this guff. Saying she's waiting for forms and I have to be vetted for the approved visitor list. But she's got so many connections. If she wanted me to see my dad, I'd be there tomorrow.'

'They're so controlling,' Clare agreed. 'I'm no swot, but I'm gonna work my butt off for the next two years, so I can get into a university as far from Locksley as I can.'

'I'm not sure my mum realises I have feelings,' John said. 'Even when she's home, she's just on her laptop, showing more love to her spreadsheets.'

Clare sighed as she rippled the sweaty shirt stuck to her skin. 'I need a shower. I'm stinking up your room.'

'I think dinner starts at six,' John said. 'We could go over together if you like.'

Clare looked coy as she got off the chair. 'Beats sitting on my own.'

'Cool,' John said, smiling. 'And feel free to use your kick-boxing on the next person who asks if I can get Robin's autograph . . .'

28. THE GREAT CASTLE HACK

Robin had his laptop under his arm as he walked into Designer Outlets' command tent, with Marion a step behind. Will Scarlock had his shirt off, because it had turned so hot, while his wife Emma drank iced tea as she sat texting with bare feet up on her desk.

'Are you two back on speaking terms?' Will asked, smiling as he glanced up from a blueprint of the mall's electrical system spread over the giant planning table. 'Should I alert security for imminent mayhem?'

Marion grinned. 'Don't worry – I'm keeping Robin on a short leash.'

'Who said it's Robin I'm worried about?' Will joked.

'Iced tea?' Emma asked, as Robin opened his new computer.

Will laughed as the laptop blazed with flickering blue and green LEDs. 'That a computer or a Christmas decoration?' he teased.

'It's state of the art,' Robin said excitedly. 'Fast RAM, mega graphics card, razor-sharp screen, but the titanium shell means it's light enough for travel.'

'Ooh, titanium . . .' Marion said, rolling her eyes. 'Swanky!'

'Be careful with it,' Emma warned, acting like a mum as she put drinks in front of Robin and Marion.

Robin wasn't mad on iced tea, but freezers were a rarity at the mall and chinking ice cubes made it wonderfully cold.

'Show us what you've got then,' Will said, coming around the table so he could see Robin's screen.

'I'm logging in via a VPN so I can't be traced back to here,' Robin explained, as he opened various programs and got a connection.

After a minute, the laptop opened an intro screen for **StayNet software VERSION 16.3**. It had an idyllic aerial shot of Sherwood Castle and the calligraphy type Sherwood Castle Resort logo. Beneath the logo were icons to open modules ranging from guest check-in, to email, staff rotas and golf.

'Looks like you've cracked it!' Will said happily.

'Not quite,' Robin said, as he clicked on the *casino* module and brought up a username and password screen. 'I got sent heaps of information last night and I've been able to use a tunnelling program to hack the castle's internet router.'

Emma was watching too and asked. 'So, this is what you'd see if you logged into the system inside the castle, at the check-in desk or a manager's office?'

'For sure.' Robin nodded, but then tapped his finger on the password box. 'Trouble is, you need staff passwords to get further. Preferably high-level ones.'

'Why high level?' Will asked.

'StayNet software has customised security levels,' Robin explained. 'A cleaner or a shop assistant probably has level-one clearance and can just access the module they need to work a checkout, or see which rooms need cleaning. But we want a password from someone senior, who has access to all the important stuff.'

'Sheriff Marjorie runs a tight ship,' Will said, as he whistled through his teeth. 'Her top people are well paid and loyal.'

'There's a weakness though,' Robin said brightly. 'The IT department also needs passwords that give full access, so they can fix any part of the system that goes wrong. So that's who I want to target.'

'How?' Will asked, as Robin drank more iced tea.

'I need to get on a computer inside Sherwood Castle,' Robin said. 'Then I can install a keylogger. I'll set it to log every keystroke made on that computer and send me a text file in an email. You can easily identify passwords because they're the first thing people type in.'

Will smiled uneasily. 'You're talking about you – Robin Hood with a bounty on his head – being inside Sherwood Castle?'

Robin nodded. 'It's a seven-hundred-room resort and casino. It's not a fortress.'

'We looked it up,' Marion added. 'You can book a room for £319 a night.'

'My concern is Robin being recognised, not the cost of a room,' Will said.

Emma nodded. 'Can't you show someone else how to install this key-log thingummy?'

'It's like Unai teaching us how to fix the roof,' Robin explained. 'I can do things he's taught me, but if anything goes wrong, you need an expert.'

'Knowing what's happening inside the castle will help us stay one step ahead of Sheriff Marjorie,' Emma said, as she exchanged a look with her husband. 'But can we put Robin in this much danger?'

'He can wear a disguise,' Marion suggested. 'He dressed like a girl when we robbed Captain Cash.'

Will rocked his head from side to side. 'I suppose, if we can find a way to stop Robin being recognised.'

'Hell yes!' Robin hooted, as Marion gave him a high five.

'Hold your horses!' Will warned. 'I'll try and work all the details out, but you two must promise that you're not going to run off again. If we decide this is too risky, that's the end of it.'

Will leaned closer to Robin and held his gaze.

'I swear,' Robin said solemnly, as Marion nodded. 'On my mum's grave.'

29. THE JOY OF FABRIC SOFTENER

The battered SUV pulling into a dark alleyway between two Nottingham apartment blocks was so old it had a *Made in Locksley* bumper sticker. Will Scarlock's nineteen-year-old son, Sam, sat in the driver's seat, with Marion alongside.

'That's her,' Marion said, as her Aunt Lucy stepped out of a battered door behind a garbage chute.

'Off you go,' Sam told her, as he pulled up. 'Take the bags.'

As Marion ran to her aunt, Sam left the engine ticking over as he walked to the back of the car. He made sure nobody else was in sight before opening the hatchback.

'Showtime, pal!' Sam said, as he whipped away a blanket.

'Stinks like something died back here,' Robin complained, as he slid out of the trunk and grabbed a backpack.

'Price of being a hero,' Sam joked, then gave Robin a friendly shove. 'Get inside and don't go doing anything crazy.'

'I'll try my best.' Robin grinned.

Sam reversed down the driveway as Robin scrambled inside, feeling disorientated. Usually when grown-ups say they're going to think about something they take forever, but once Will spoke to Indio and agreed that Robin's plan made sense, they'd pulled everything together in three days.

'Top floor,' Lucy said, as Robin stepped into a bare concrete stairwell, with flies circling a burst bin bag.

Marion had raced ahead, but Robin stayed with Lucy. He'd not met her before and thought she looked like an older, chunkier version of her sister, Indio.

'Thanks for letting me use your den these past months,' Robin told her politely.

'You're very welcome,' Lucy smiled. 'Have you eaten all my hot sauce?'

The den had three shelves lined with Lucy's hot-sauce collection and he laughed at the thought.

'Otto dared Matt to try your Habanero Monster and it made him puke! Me and Marion practically died laughing.'

Lucy laughed as they rounded a landing. 'I miss my crazy nephews!'

'Karma and Indio would probably let you have 'em,' Robin joked.

By this time they'd reached the door of the third-floor apartment Lucy shared with her partner, Seb. The one-bed apartment was cramped and smelled like body spray. The washer and dryer were in a cupboard inside the entrance and Marion was already down on her knees pulling mounds of dirty clothes out of her bag.

'I know dryers and chemicals are bad for the environment,' she explained to Robin. 'But at the mall my clothes never come out soft. And everything gets washed with my brothers' stuff, so half the time it comes out smelling worse than it went in.'

Lucy unscrewed the lid on a fancy little bottle of fabric conditioner. 'I got this for you,' she told Marion, then read from the packaging. '*Succulent Fuchsia Blossom with Scent Blast technology.* It's supposed to keep clothes smelling nice for five or six washes.'

As Marion sniffed her fabric conditioner and told Lucy she was the best auntie ever, Robin walked down a short hallway to the living room. Lucy's partner Seb sat in a rattan chair with Sony headphones and a crime novel.

'The legendary Mr Hood!' Seb said dramatically, as he got up to shake Robin's hand.

Seb looked ten years too young to be Lucy's boyfriend and everything about him was long. Long arms, long nose, long hair and long bony feet minus one big toe.

'Snake bit me in the forest,' Seb explained when he caught Robin looking at it.

Once everyone had drinks and Marion's washing was churning, Seb told Robin to stand in the middle of the living room with arms straight at his sides. At the same time, Lucy went into the bedroom and came back with three designer-brand carrier bags filled with boys' clothes.

'How much did this lot cost?' Marion asked, clearly jealous as she peered into a Ralph Lauren bag.

'Don't sweat it,' Lucy said, as her niece fished out a pair of trendy black jeans. 'I run the Animal Freedom Militia campaign office here in Nottingham. 'I've set up brilliant fundraising teams at all the big universities, and someone recently left us a nice donation in their will.'

'These would fit me,' Marion hinted, holding the jeans up in front of her legs.

'Stealing from a charity?' Robin said, grinning. 'Despicable!'

Lucy smiled as she took the jeans and threw them towards Marion's backpack.

'Must have lost that pair . . .' Lucy said, as Marion looked chuffed.

Robin was starting to feel weird with his arms by his sides and Seb moving around, staring like he was a sculpture.

'Indio told me your background was theatre costumes,' Robin said.

Seb made a tiny nod and snort, like he was a great artist who shouldn't be disturbed.

'This long scruffy hair is versatile,' he announced finally. 'I can easily cut it to a different look. You have broad shoulders too, so I can sew padding into a vest and make you fatter, without your body looking out of proportion.

'I'm thinking some glasses with clear lenses, and for clothes a preppy rich-kid look. Chinos, striped shirt, lambswool sweater around your neck and smart casual shoes. But that filthy backpack of yours doesn't fit the part.'

'I didn't think about bags,' Lucy said, sounding frustrated. 'But the shops open at ten, so I can pick something up.'

'And no bow,' Seb said. 'That's a huge giveaway.'

'Indio made me leave it at Designer Outlets,' Robin said, trying to ignore Seb combing fingers through his hair. 'I feel naked without it, but I've got a little stun gun Flash took from Agnes McIntyre when . . .'

He broke off, embarrassed, so Marion finished his sentence.

'When this twerp ran off and almost got himself killed,' she said.

'Hey!' Robin snapped.

Marion gave Robin the finger and he couldn't retaliate because he was standing to attention for Seb.

'This hair is so greasy you could cook chips in it!' Seb told Robin. 'You need to shower and shampoo before

I can cut. Use the conditioner in the gold bottle and leave it in for at least ten minutes.'

'I wonder if we could sell locks of Robin's hair after you chop it?' Lucy said, laughing at her own joke as Robin sat on a pouffe and started untying his boots. 'He's a famous outlaw, after all.'

'Auntie, no!' Marion snapped, shaking her head but half-smiling. 'Robin's ego is big enough, without you encouraging him!'

30. FAKE BELLY AND SPECS

'Try not to get killed,' Marion suggested, when Robin and Lucy left the apartment before noon the next day.

Robin's real stomach was tense, while the fake one stuffed with the contents of a polyester pillow felt hot under his shirt. He also had brown leather boat shoes, glasses that made him sore behind both ears and short gelled hair.

Seb had also transformed Lucy, from ponytail, leggings and singlet, to beach waves, designer dress and leather bag with matching wheelie case.

To decrease the risk of being tracked back to the apartment, Robin and Lucy rode a tram out to Nottingham Airport. From there they walked to arrivals and met a pre-booked chauffeur, who asked how their flight had been as he took them to a parked BMW.

After a speedy ride along Route 24, they stopped at a sinister checkpoint staffed by armed Castle Guards, then passed a convoy of Rolls-Royces going the other way on a private road hemmed by mesh fence and security cameras.

Sheriff Marjorie had used government grants, huge loans and her bulldozer personality to transform Sherwood Castle from an ivy-clad ruin into a lavish forest resort, with casino, golf courses, conference centre, managed hunting and five-star hotel.

As Lucy and Robin stepped out of the BMW, a doorperson fought the chauffeur to grab luggage, two tartan-suited staff opened lobby doors and at check-in a super-smiley clerk was backed up by a lobby boy offering fruit-infused water or Japanese green tea.

While Robin wondered if the yellow-and-blue angelfish in the vast aquarium behind the reception desk were as bored as they looked, Lucy got a twinge of nerves as she handed over a driving licence and credit card in a false name.

'That's a key card each for you and your son, Mrs Newman,' the receptionist said. 'Room 814. Your package includes a complimentary casino chip, so good luck at the tables and I hope you enjoy your stay!'

They headed up to the eighth floor in a glass lift that overlooked an atrium filled with fountains and rows of flashing slot machines around the casino entrance.

'This place is massive,' Robin said, as he gawped through the glass. 'No wonder it cost half a billion.'

'Don't stare,' Lucy warned. 'We're classy people! We're supposed to belong here.'

'Not bad,' Robin said, as they stepped into their plush hotel room, with a huge TV, fresh flowers, a pair of double beds and a large window with an underwhelming view over air-conditioning units.

'Are you set?' Lucy asked, as Robin somersaulted on the bed, then ploughed head first into cushions and pillows.

'I need to stroll and check things out,' Robin said, as he rolled onto his back. 'Will's source gave me pointers on where to find unattended computers. He said there's a nightclub and golf shop that are only manned when they're open, plus terminals behind desks in the conference centre.'

'Can I do anything?'

Robin shook his head. 'Just what we planned. You head to the casino. Kids can't go in there, so if security or anyone asks why I'm wandering around, I'm a bored kid waiting for my mum to finish gambling. Once I've decided which computer I'm gonna hack, I'll come back to this room and let Freya Tuck know where it is and what time she's needed.'

'Do you want to grab lunch first?'

Robin thought for a second. 'The longer I'm out of the room, the more chance I'll be recognised.'

'Seb did a great job,' Lucy pointed out. 'I'd be *amazed* if anyone recognised you looking the way you do.'

'Let's hope,' Robin said. 'But it's still safest if I come back here, and I've never stayed in a hotel or ordered room service before.'

Lucy smiled. 'Not ever?'

'We never had much money,' Robin explained. 'Plus, my dad's idea of a holiday usually involved walking halfway up a mountain and pitching our leaky tent.'

31. TOO MUCH FOOD

Five hours after check-in Robin sat on the hotel bed with his shirt off, a touch queasy after scoffing a huge room-service burger and peach milkshake, followed by a pecan brownie with hot chocolate sauce.

He checked the time and had started reattaching the Velcro straps that stopped his fake belly from sliding around when his phone rang.

Will Scarlock's voice was a surprise. 'You OK?'

'So far, so good,' Robin said.

'I just spoke to Freya. She's in a taxi and should be inside the castle with Lyla in around ten minutes. How did the scouting go?'

'There's an amusement arcade near the casino entrance where parents dump kids,' Robin said. 'I played pinball for twenty minutes to make my plight look realistic. Then I wandered around checking . . .' He paused to burp. 'Sorry,' he said. 'Just ate a burger.'

Will laughed. 'I can't eat when I'm nervous.'

'I get more excited than nervous,' Robin said.

'Fear is healthy because it protects us from danger,' Will warned. 'Nobody is going to hold anything against you if you sense danger and pull out.'

'I know,' Robin said firmly. 'The castle is quieter than I thought it would be. I wandered around for an hour. The restaurants were all dead. I saw maybe two security officers, some people checking in and a few people with golf trolleys.'

'I'll let you get on,' Will said. 'Keep safe and see you safely back here tomorrow.'

Robin finished strapping on his belly and buttoned his shirt over it, then took a pee and grabbed his new backpack. He only needed a USB stick, screwdriver set and a little fold-out keyboard for the hack, but he took all his stuff because he didn't want things left behind if something went wrong.

He was halfway out the door when a message from Freya pinged Robin's phone.

Just arrived with Lyla. Ready when you are.

As he rode down in the elevator Robin regretted eating so much. He'd decided to target a pair of food counters in a recess near the huge lobby fountains. One was a coffee shop, the other sold Italian ice cream, and they both had signs saying that they closed at six thirty.

It was now seven, so the coffee shop had its shutters down, while the ice-cream counter had lights off, and a silver-grey canopy pulled over the tubs of ice cream in the glass-topped freezer.

Robin sat on the black marble plinth edging the fountains. The atrium was busier than earlier, with guests heading to dinner, or the casino. Spanish guitar music wafted while a young girl tried to reach in and grab coins out of the water. As the girl's dad plucked her up and told her off, Robin sighted Freya and Lyla.

They'd have stuck out at Sherwood Castle in grubby forest gear, so they'd made a dinner reservation and put on dresses and make-up. Robin didn't make eye contact but folded his arms to indicate he was ready. Freya fiddling with her watch was the signal that she'd heard him.

Robin pretended to play with his phone, but kept glancing up at the ice-cream stand and the two young women.

'You did WHAT!' Lyla screamed suddenly, loud enough to make people stop and look.

'It's nothing to do with you!' Freya shouted back.

'I'll give you nothing, donkey face!' Lyla yelled, then gave Freya a mighty two-handed shove.

The plan called for the pair to cause the biggest distraction possible and he thought it was a nice touch when Lyla ripped a fire extinguisher off the wall.

There were around thirty people nearby and every eye locked on the brawling women as Lyla squeezed the extinguisher, blitzing Freya with white powder.

'I'll rip your head off!' Freya yelled, as she fought clouds of carbon dioxide and made out like she was going for Lyla's throat.

A bystander tried to separate them, but got his golf attire blasted, while Freya shot off and hurdled into the ankle-deep pool around the fountains.

Robin was so startled by the fire-extinguisher stunt that he momentarily forgot it was all for his benefit.

As everyone watched Freya charging through the fountains yelling, 'I hate you so much!' while Lyla chased after blasting the fire extinguisher, nobody saw Robin make a brisk walk and slide over the ice-cream counter.

32. CRUSHED NUTS

Robin landed behind the counter without hurting himself, but he was jarred by the space's similarity to the sandwich counter he'd dived behind at Seven Stars Services. It surely couldn't go any worse than that . . .

The floor was sticky with dropped ice cream and trampled M&M's, and the smell of crushed nuts and strawberry sauce was unwelcome after his giant meal.

Robin located the compact PC on a shelf below a cash drawer. It was linked to a touchscreen built into the countertop. There was no keyboard or mouse, so he took the folding travel keyboard out of his pack and plugged it into a USB port.

Sometimes companies disable USB ports to prevent hacking, so Robin was relieved when tapping the space bar made the computer kick out of standby.

'Saves me some work,' Robin murmured, as he plugged a USB memory stick into another slot, then went up on one knee so he could read the screen in the countertop.

The computer had come out of standby, but the touchscreen just showed rectangular menu boxes for different types of ice cream and payment methods. It took Robin thirty frustrating seconds to navigate his way out of the StayNet payment system and onto a regular desktop.

Once he had a screen of desktop icons, he found the folder for his USB drive and clicked an icon to install his keylogger program. But a box popped up on screen:

Administrator Password Required to Install

Robin didn't have an administrator login, but it was a problem he knew how to fix.

After closing the warning box, he clicked on another item on his USB drive. The file opened inside the computer's internet browser, then ran a script that exploited a flaw in the operating system to give the browser administrator-level access.

Robin opened the keylogger file from inside the web browser and a menu popped up asking if he wanted to install it. After clicking *yes*, he clicked *OK* on a box warning him that unverified software could damage the computer. Then he closed the browser and was chuffed to see an icon for the keylogger program on the desktop.

Robin opened the keylogger, tapped random keys to see that it was registering every keystroke, then opened a settings menu. He set the program to run every time the computer was switched on, and to send him an email every hour containing everything that had been typed.

Robin was grabbing a multibit screwdriver set out of his pack when he was distracted by men shouting. As he peeked over the counter, he saw that Freya and Lyla had stopped fighting. The pair now stood in the fountain with their dresses soaked, while three burly security officers barked orders for them to come out.

'Come and get us!' Lyla taunted, as she kicked up a spray of water.

But none of the guards wanted to get their fancy tweed suits wet.

Robin smirked as he powered the computer down and slid it away from its shelf. It was awkward balancing the warm dusty box, so he dragged a plastic waste bin from beneath the counter and rested it on top of that.

Three Torx screws held the computer's lid in place. Robin slotted a star-shaped bit into his screwdriver, freed the screws and slid off the metal panel to expose the interior. Computers often have thick dust inside, but this one was only months old and mostly clean.

Robin had learned a lot about repairing computers from his dad, so he knew what all the components inside did.

The main processor in a computer gets hot, so fans blow cool air through the case to stop it overheating. A broken fan is one of the most common faults a computer can have, and Robin reached inside with his screwdriver and used the pointy end to break wires in the cable linking the fan to the power supply.

After replacing the lid, tightening the three screws and sliding the computer back onto its shelf, Robin pressed the power button. There was no whirr from the fan, and when the computer detected that it wasn't working, it made a loud beep, before shutting down everything except a blinking red error light next to the power button.

When the ice-cream sellers arrived for work in the morning, they'd find a dead computer and make a call to the IT department.

33. SOGGY DRESSES

With the phishing operation completed, Robin put everything back in his pack, slung it on his back, then stood up and almost died from a heart attack.

While Robin had been disconnecting the fan inside the computer, the hotel manager had arrived by the fountains and ordered her security staff to wade into the water and grab the two young women.

Freya and Lyla knew they risked serious consequences if they attacked anyone apart from each other, so when two beefy guards finally stepped into the water, the crowd was disappointed by the pair's meek surrender.

'I don't know what came over me,' Freya said, as she wrapped her arms around a startled guard and began fake sobbing. 'She's my best friend. We got carried away.'

'It's my eighteenth birthday,' Lyla wailed. 'We ruined a special night.'

'I'm so embarrassed . . .' Freya sniffed, as a guard picked her missing shoe out of the water.

The manager spoke into her radio. 'Front desk, I want a clean-up crew and four bath towels.'

The guards looked awkward, with soggy trouser legs and two hysterical teenagers dripping everywhere and blocking the path around the lobby fountains.

The manager glanced about, not sure where they could go until she saw the little alcove with a shuttered coffee shop and ice cream counter . . .

So as Robin stood up to slide back over the counter, a shivering Freya and Lyla arrived on the other side.

He dived back down, almost flat to the floor, because the counter was glass and Freya, Lyla, three security guards and the hotel manager were right there.

Towels were brought by housekeeping and a guard brought plastic chairs for Freya and Lyla to sit on.

Robin looked for a way out. There was a door with a fire-exit sign at the back of the counter, but he had no idea where it went, or if an alarm would sound when he pushed it.

Once the girls had towelled off the worst of the fountain water, the manager stood with hands on hips to have a go at them.

'It seems the only damage is an empty fire extinguisher, so I'm giving you ladies a choice,' she growled. 'I can make copies of your ID, ban you from ever coming back to Sherwood Castle and put you in a taxi. Or I can call the cops.'

As Freya and Lyla obediently let the manager snap photos of their fake identity cards, one of the guards who'd been in the fountain was hunting for something to clean his glasses.

'There's a tissue dispenser over there,' the guard who'd fetched the chairs said, pointing to the wall at the end of the ice-cream counter.

Robin gulped, then crab-walked backwards to the fire door, thinking he'd have to charge through and hope for the best. But the guard had long arms and stretched over to tear off a length of tissue without stepping behind the counter, or turning his head and seeing Robin less than three metres away.

Robin stayed on edge, but now things went his way. The manager ordered the two guards who'd been in the fountain to go and change in the staff locker room, while the third escorted Freya and Lyla to a taxi rank in front of the main entrance.

Finally the manager picked up the empty fire extinguisher and damp towels. Robin sat up slightly as she headed out of the alcove. There was a cleaner drying the plinth around the fountains, but he was facing the water, so Robin decided to risk it.

He squeaked over the counter and strode out into the atrium.

Though there were plenty of people around as Robin started walking, none of them noticed where he'd come from. But the close call had spooked him and he got chills down his back thinking about the security cameras in the ceiling and expecting the hand of some plain-clothes Castle Guard on his shoulder.

Robin reached the glass lifts without really thinking where he was going, then leaned against a wall and phoned Lucy.

'Is it done?' she asked. 'All good?'

'Could have been worse,' Robin said. 'But this place is giving me the creeps. I want to get out of here.'

'No reason to stay,' Lucy agreed. 'I'll meet you in the lobby in five.'

34. UP WITH THE COCK

Robin didn't get back from Sherwood Castle until midnight. He'd hoped to get a morning off, but Will showed no mercy and as the sun rose he was on Designer Outlets' roof, collecting eggs, scraping poop and filling trays with dried feed and bundles of fresh weeds that Chicken Sheila picked in the mall parking lot.

Although Robin hated getting up early, he'd grown fond of the birds, who chased him affectionately around the runs because they knew he brought breakfast. He'd even stopped eating chicken because he thought of them whenever he saw it on his plate.

After finishing his shift and disinfecting his boots, Robin slid out his phone and checked the email address he'd set up for the keylogger. It was only eight and he doubted anyone would spot the faulty PC until the Sherwood Castle ice-cream counter opened at ten, but he was anxious enough to check anyway.

He checked again after he'd swapped grubby work clothes for shorts and T-shirt in his den. He checked as

Karma dished up scrambled eggs on toast for breakfast. Checked after he'd eaten them. Checked as he sat on the toilet and as he walked to his 10 a.m. study session in the shuttered branch of Bargain Book Bonanza on the first floor.

About forty school-age kids lived in the mall, from little ones learning their ABC, to Freya Tuck aiming for university. Fortunately, the bargain book outlet had little alcoves, so kids could split into study groups. And while there was no qualified teacher, a few parents always stuck around to prevent anarchy.

Robin and Marion, plus Matt and his pal Raiden, sat on a rug in what had been the Arts & Music section, studying a home-school module on the Balkans War.

As an ancient laptop showed video of prisoners behind barbed wire and Nighthawk bomber raids, Matt and Raiden stuck pencils up their noses, Marion completed an overdue maths homework, and Robin pulled his phone to check for the thousandth time.

A stocky parent called Mr Khan, with a black beard and a kufi cap, swooped out of nowhere. 'You know the rules,' he roared triumphantly. 'No phone for you!'

'Just moving it,' Robin lied. 'It was digging in my leg.'

'Give!' Mr Khan said, reaching out. 'You'll have it back when we finish at twelve thirty.'

Robin fumed. The ice-cream shop was open now, so he could get a message from the keylogger at any time.

'It's for something important,' Robin said.

Mr Khan's eyes popped as he leaned closer and pointed out towards the mall. 'You may think you're special, Robin Hood. But in class, you follow rules like everyone else.'

'You're not special, Robin,' Matt parroted sarcastically.

Marion snapped at her brother. 'Next time you stick a pencil up your snout, I might punch it the rest of the way into your tiny brain!'

Robin *really* wanted to keep his phone. But Mr Khan wasn't backing down, and next ninety minutes felt like a million years.

'And?' Marion asked, when Robin finally got his phone back.

Robin beamed when he saw a little envelope in his notifications. He opened an email with a short text file attachment and sprinted off without answering.

Marion chased Robin down to Designer Outlets' first floor and into the sports store but didn't bother following him up the escalator.

'You left your laptop charging down here,' she yelled, but

Robin didn't hear.

He looked annoyed when he stumbled breathlessly into the Maid family den, where Marion waited by his computer with a smug grin.

Karma was asleep on a futon, but Indio came to watch as Robin logged in.

'What have we got?' she asked.

Robin scanned the keylogger text. There were only six lines, beginning with lots of F8 and arrow-key presses, which he recognised as someone clicking through a set-up menu. Then there was an email 'nadine@sherwood.castle' and a string of characters that had to be a password.

'Here goes,' Robin said eagerly, as he tunnelled the Sherwood Castle internet router and entered Nadine's password. After a pause a whole bunch of extra options appeared in a panel on the right, with names like **Advanced Settings** and **Create User**.

'I think it worked,' he said happily, as he clicked on the *golf* module. Now, instead of the password screen, a menu flashed up with images of the castle's three golf courses and a list showing who was currently playing and who was booked in for the afternoon.

When Robin clicked on a player named Robert Wharton, it took him to a screen showing Wharton's room number, his check-in and check-out dates and more detailed information, like a breakfast order, his home address and that he'd lost £650 in the casino the night before.

'Nice work, kiddo,' Indio said, as she kissed Robin's cheek. 'Do you think you can use this to find out when Sheriff Marjorie's big trophy hunt is happening?'

'Maybe,' Robin said thoughtfully.

He exited back to the StayNet menu and found a module called *Events & Conference*. A list scrolled up showing hundreds of events, from wedding chapel bookings to a showcase for a leather goods importer.

Indio and Robin looked disappointed, but Marion had noticed something.

'Scroll back, there's a gap,' she said.

'Eh?' Robin said.

'In the calendar,' Marion explained. 'Every day has heaps of events, but there's three days in two weekends' time with nothing at all.'

Robin saw it, then switched from the *events* module to *guest reservations*. When he clicked *June 13th* a list of hundreds of hotel rooms popped up.

'Tap where it says *VIP Suites*,' Marion suggested.

They all gasped at the list of names. A royal couple, an Arab prince, two film stars, one pop star and . . .

'That's the hunt,' Indio said, then read two names aloud, 'Richard King III and John King. The founder of King Corporation and his brother.'

'I've only scratched the surface,' Robin said proudly. 'There's heaps of other modules I can dig into. Purchasing, staff rotas . . .'

'What's your favourite dinner, Robin?' Indio asked. 'You're getting it tonight, even if we have to send someone to Locksley to buy ingredients!'

Marion looked at Robin and cracked a mischievous smile. 'How about roast chicken?'

PART IV
THIRTEEN DAYS LATER

35. FRIENDS AND FRENEMIES

'That practice was a gosh-darned disgrace!' Barnsdale School's head rugby coach shouted, as thirty exhausted lads sauntered off a sun-blitzed school pitch. 'Too much la-de-dah cricket! You boys are getting soft on me!'

Little John was sweaty and breathless as he dropped a rugby ball into a net and his red training bib on a pile.

'You're fast for a big guy,' the coach told John, as she jogged up. 'But you have to practise footwork. At this level, even a monster like you can't expect to just charge in a straight line and knock people down like skittles.'

'Yes, coach,' John gasped.

'If I show you some footwork drills next time, will you practise over summer?'

'Yes, coach.'

'And wear sunscreen. You've caught your neck and brow.'

'Yes, coach.'

John pulled off his boots then entered the noise and stink of the changing room. When he sat down, he felt pains down his thighs and swelling where a boot stud scraped his ribs. The other guys were all bantering, and John felt even more awkward than usual, because he'd been at Barnsdale for three weeks while most of them had played together for years.

He pulled his team shirt and body armour off in one, and as his head emerged an olive-skinned fly-half called Rui sat alongside him on the changing bench.

'You're red, fella!' Rui said cheerfully.

John wiped his face with his shirt and nodded. 'I didn't realise how bright it was.'

'So, Hood,' Rui said, 'us lads gonna party tonight. We hang out by the boating lake, play some sounds, invite lots of ladies. Are you in?'

John liked that everyone called him Hood, despite his mother's attempt to stick him with Kovacevic. He was less sure about partying.

'What about curfew?'

Rui laughed. 'Staff turn a blind eye if it's not too wild. And you can invite Clare.'

'Tell her to bring her soccer pals,' someone added, from deep in the shower steam.

'No!' someone else shouted. 'Those soccer girls are crazy! Remember Easter, when they drank all our beer, then sat on Mark and shaved his eyebrows off?'

'We *want* crazy girls!' Rui said, looking at John. 'That's the best kind, right?'

'All girls are nice,' John said weakly.

Rui nodded. 'You're always with Clare. Is it boyfriend and girlfriend?'

'We go back a long way,' John said. 'I suppose we're friends now . . .'

'You ain't gonna whine if I work my manly charm with Clare tonight?' Rui asked.

Several boys laughed when they heard this, and a dripping lump called Eugene closed up wearing just a towel.

'Face facts, Rui,' he began. 'First, you've got no charm. Second, you're ugly. Third, Clare Gisborne is the only daughter of a badass gangster. Any sane dude would steer well clear of that!'

Laughter and shouts of *burn* erupted around the locker room.

Rui's shoulders and face tightened, but Eugene was twice his size and his comeback was a feeble, 'What do you know, meathead?'

The Rui–Eugene face-off ended as attention switched to a kid that tripped as he walked to the shower. As roars and laughter erupted again, Rui turned back to John.

'Are you in for tonight, or what?'

John found parties awkward, but wanted to fit in with his new teammates.

'I guess,' John said. 'But I probably won't stay late. My ma's got a big event this weekend and the helicopter's picking me up first thing.'

Rui held out a palm. 'So, it's twenty each.'

John looked baffled. 'Twenty what?'

'Pounds,' Rui said, like John was stupid. 'For beer. It's all set up. A guy from the village drops it off by the lake, but everyone has to pay their share.

John felt conned. 'I don't have cash on me.'

'The Rich List says your ma's worth eighty million, so I guess you're good for it.'

'I'll pay you on Monday,' John agreed.

'Good man,' Rui said cheerfully. 'And remember, get Clare to invite her soccer pals.'

36. VITAL SANDWICH PRODUCTION

Marion, Indio and Freya stood by the kitchen counter in the Maid family den, while Robin, Matt and Otto sat on cushions a few metres away playing Mario Kart.

Indio buttered slices from a big stack of sliced bread, Freya added grated cheese, tomato and lettuce, before Marion finished the production line by cutting each sandwich in half and wrapping it in tinfoil.

'*Please* can I come, Mum?' Marion begged. 'I've wanted to go on an AFM operation my whole life, and I'm thirteen in two weeks!'

'It's too risky,' Indio said. 'In a couple of years . . .'

Marion groaned. 'But Robin's going!'

Indio twisted her face awkwardly. 'I know that seems unfair, but Robin is a special case.'

Across the room, Matt crashed Bowser into a wall, thumped his controller against the floor and yelled, 'Every time on that *stupid* corner.'

Otto screamed, 'Three–nil, I am the king!' as he won the race, while Robin came a distant third and had too much else on his mind to care.

'Cut the racket, boys,' Indio ordered, before looking back at Marion. 'Robin is coming because our campaign will get ten times more publicity if he's involved.'

'He'd better not get separated is all,' Marion said sourly. 'I've never known anyone with a crummier sense of direction.'

Robin looked around, ready to make a sarcastic comment, but Marion's dark scowl made him think better of it. As the next Mario Kart race started, Azeem entered the den. She looked terrifying, with her beefy frame in full combat gear and a forest-slashing machete strapped to her belt.

'The two vets have arrived and they're heading down to south mall,' she said. 'How are you lot doing?'

'We've done breakfasts, so just a few cheese sandwiches to make,' Freya said.

'Robin, have you got plenty of water?' Indio nagged.

'Three litres,' Robin said, as he deliberately drove his cart into lava and quit playing.

'And the action cameras?'

'For the fifth time,' Robin said wearily, 'I've charged them up and we have spare batteries if they die.'

It took a few minutes to make the rest of the sandwiches, then bag them up with apples and energy bars.

'OK, boys,' Indio yelled. 'Mummy, Freya and Robin are leaving now. Pause that game and get over here.'

Matt and Otto straddled the mounded cushions and Indio squatted down and eyeballed them. 'Will and Emma are looking after Finn. But Karma is suffering in this heat, so I *seriously* need you two to behave.'

'Yes, Mum,' they droned, as Freya helped Robin pull on a hefty backpack.

Indio looked at Marion. 'You're the boss while Karma's resting. If these two muck about, you have my personal authorisation to sit on their heads and fart.'

'What?!' Otto blurted, as Marion grinned and pounded a fist into her palm. 'Wait . . . Is that a joke?'

Matt gave the kind of special tut reserved for big brothers who know better. 'Of course Mum's joking, you thicko.'

Once everyone who was leaving had their packs on, they started hugging.

'Be safe, Mum,' Marion said, then to Freya. 'Love you, cuz.'

Robin felt awkward as Marion approached. 'If I was in charge, you'd be with us,' he said.

Marion whispered, 'I spat in your sandwich,' but hugged him anyway.

She felt a tear in her eye as Azeem, Freya, Robin and her mum headed out. As soon as they were out of sight, Matt and Otto bolted for the door.

'Hey!' Marion yelled.

'Meeting our boys at the food court,' Matt said, breaking into a sprint in case his sister tried to grab. 'Don't wait up.'

Marion shook her head, then turned and groaned as she saw the kitchen cabinet still covered in bread, dirty cutlery, an open mayo jar and a million scraps of grated cheese and lettuce.

'Don't worry about me,' she moaned to herself. 'You all go off and have an adventure. I *love* staying here picking up your mess . . .'

37. SOUTH END SHOOT-OUT

Sherwood Designer Outlets was laid out like an H, with the glass-domed food court bridging two long arcades of shops. Everyone lived in the top part of the H, because drains at the southern end had choked with silt from the nearby river. Water swept through every time it rained, and after a big storm the south mall's ground floor could stay underwater for days.

Sun on the skylights turned this abandoned area into a steamy greenhouse. There were clumps of glossy black fungus that kids liked to burst with sticks, while climbing plants grew up columns and weaved between railings on the upper walkway.

Robin hated the damp smell and pulled the neck of his shirt over his nose as he followed Azeem over the puddled floor. He was worried about the weight in his pack. He was strong for his age and could run for ages, but he still struggled to keep up with people who regularly did long treks through the forest.

The first stop was Eldridge's Depot. This huge department-store outlet once anchored the mall's southern end, and after Robin ducked under the plastic entrance grille, he looked up at an atrium with escalators rising four floors and gulls nesting at the base of a column of light where a section of roof had caved.

Fresh air cleared the mouldy smell as Freya, Robin, Azeem and Indio walked briskly up a frozen escalator. There were six others waiting for them. Lyla, Lucy, Seb, a young couple who were both qualified vets and a professional videographer who was crouching low to film Robin's arrival.

This floor had been womenswear, and Robin counted eight clothing dummies set up in a row.

'Good, good, we're all here!' Lucy began cheerfully. 'Whenever I give a talk before an Animal Freedom Militia raid, I always say I feel like Princess Leia, sending the rebels to destroy the Death Star.'

Weak laughter came from the group.

'But this time we're taking on Sherwood Castle, which really is the Death Star of Sherwood Forest. Now, I'm not going into massive detail, because you all know where we're going and your roles when we get there.

'But most of you aren't familiar with the paintball guns we'll be using, so we'll go through that now, with a little help from our ladies across the room.'

Robin was buzzing as everyone took paintball guns from a wooden rack. But by the time he'd also been given goggles, a spare gas cylinder and two large tubs of red paintballs, he was more concerned about the extra weight.

Once they all had their equipment, Lucy began by explaining how to fit the gas cylinder, load the ammunition balls and fix jams and air leaks.

'Most important of all, safety!' Lucy said, as she placed an apple on a display plinth.

She shot it with a paintball from one metre and the apple exploded.

'Paintballs can do damage at close range,' she warned. 'The Animal Freedom Militia's objective is to show the horrible conditions animals are kept in at Sherwood Castle, stop the trophy hunt and shame the hunters. But we'll lose public support if someone is blinded, or shot in the mouth and chokes.

'So don't shoot anyone from under three metres, don't aim higher than a person's nipples and don't shoot wildly if there isn't an obvious target.

'Finally, remember that most of us will be wearing action cameras and we're going to try and live-stream the raid if we can get a good signal. So no bloody swearing!'

After a few more laughs Lucy asked who wanted to try their gun first.

'None of you?' Lucy said, disappointed. 'Well, Robin has a reputation for sharpshooting, so let's see what he can do.'

Robin was a quick learner, but he'd never shot a paintball gun before and felt nervy, with everyone watching and the eager cameraman stepping around to film his first shots. He aimed down the gunsight and held his breath like when he shot his bow.

From ten metres, Robin's first shot hit the central dummy in the front of the neck with a satisfying red splat. He was pleased with the result, so he aimed up and shot twice in quick succession, hitting between the eyes with enough force to make the dummy crash over backwards.

He lowered the gun and turned around smiling, but was surprised to see awkward expressions and Lucy looking furious.

'Delete that now!' Lucy yelled to the cameraman, then turned towards Robin shaking her head. 'What did I *just* say about shooting people in the face?'

'Oh, right!' Robin said guiltily. 'I know, but it's only a dummy . . .'

'We haven't got all day and I guess we at least know Robin can shoot straight,' she said irritably. 'Now, who wants to try next?'

38. RUGBY BOYZ PAR-TAY

About thirty rugby players snuck out of their dorms just after nine. The organisers located their illicit stash of beer in woodland on the edge of school grounds and met up with the rest in the parking lot behind Barnsdale School's swanky maple-clad boathouse.

A boombox blasted rock and rap as shouty lads chugged beers, bragged, boasted, tossed rugby balls around and fought for the attention of the modest number of females who'd decided that this was how they wanted to spend a Friday night.

Clare Gisborne was in her element. She drank every beer handed to her and drew cheers as she wrecked the egos of two rugby players who made the mistake of challenging her to a wrestling match. A third earned a fat lip for the sexist comment he made as she rolled around on the ground.

But it was closer to Little John's idea of hell. He stayed on the edge of the gathering, sipping his first beer until the tin grew warm. When he wandered off into trees where lads were peeing, he kept going until he reached reeds at the edge of the huge artificial lake.

He spent ages watching ducks cruising in the moonlight, but it took a rare moment of quiet in the mayhem by the boathouse to hear girls laughing on a wooden pontoon less than ten metres away.

John's face went hot when he realised how close they were. He had a horrible feeling they'd think he was some weirdo who'd been staring at them, but the ground was soft this close to the water and his shoe squelched as he turned away.

It was only mud on one knee and the palm he put down to save himself, but a pretty barefoot girl came running. John knew she was called Amber because she was in his art class, though he'd never spoken to her.

'Are you OK?' she asked.

'Just muddy,' John said, as she scrambled up.

'We saw you staring at the water,' she said. 'Not enjoying the party?'

John shrugged. 'Not really my scene.'

Amber led him back to the pontoon. Two more girls sat with their feet in the water, and John liked the way the moonlight caught their skin. They said hello, but let Amber do the talking.

As John swished his hand through the water and rubbed his knee to wash off the mud, she explained that they came out here once or twice a week when it was warm, just sitting around chatting or playing with their phones to get away from the noise in their dorm.

'And then my rugby mates pile out here and ruin it,' John said. 'Sorry!'

John and the three girls spent ages talking. He felt annoyed when Robin got mentioned, but overcame his shyness as he told a story about his little brother being sad after his mum died, and how he climbed out of a third-storey window and perched on top of a roof.

'Robin had only just turned seven. Adults kept saying his mum was up in heaven, and he told my dad he'd climbed up so he could be closer to her.'

'That is so sweet,' Amber said, as the other two made *Aww* sounds.

John was enjoying having the three girls paying him lots of attention and started another anecdote.

'Robin was always wild,' he said. 'When he first started getting into archery, he saw a video about flaming arrows. So, in the middle of the summer holidays, he persuaded me to film him setting fire to arrows and shooting them at the mailbox of an abandoned house.

'Every time the arrow hit the mailbox, the flame snuffed out. So Robin stuffed the mailbox with dry grass soaked in petrol from the can my dad used to fill his lawnmower.'

'Oh my God!' Amber gasped.

'It made a huge fireball!' John said, shaking his arms dramatically. 'I was filming and it crisped all the hairs up my arm.'

'You could have been really hurt,' Amber said.

'Obviously,' John said. 'Kids do stupid things . . .'

'Did you get in trouble?'

John shook his head. 'Not really. There were whole streets of abandoned houses around where we lived in Locksley. The fire didn't spread beyond a patch of burned grass, and we wiped the video because our dad would have murdered us if he'd seen it.'

'You must worry about Robin,' Amber said sympathetically.

John nodded. 'We don't have much in common, but I do love him.'

John felt sad as he said this, then excited when Amber shuffled up a little closer and gently stroked the back of his hand. He briefly made eye contact and it felt like the moment in a movie where people kiss. Except it wasn't, because her two friends were way too close and then there was a radical change in the noise coming from around the boathouse.

The music had stopped and there was wild animal moaning. Someone was in a lot of pain and everyone else seemed to be gasping and running away.

'Sounds like they're getting busted,' one of Amber's pals said, as she pulled her feet out of the water and reached for her sandals.

'We'd better shift out of here,' Amber agreed.

39. YOU'RE GONNA CARRY THAT WEIGHT

The forest canopy shaded the heat, but with drones patrolling the sky and a forest full of informants, the group of ten had to avoid popular routes. Fresh spring growth meant regular halts while Seb and Azeem used machetes to clear their path.

The two vets – Chris and Adrianna – were new to the forest and had a tough time, but it was Robin who had the heaviest pack relative to his size and kept falling behind. After two hours striding north, Freya and Lyla took pity and Robin felt ashamed as they took stuff out of his pack to make life easier.

'I'm sorry,' he gasped.

'Just make us look good when you write your autobiography,' Lyla joked.

'And give us a cut of the money,' Freya added.

There were ten kilometres between Designer Outlets and Sherwood Castle on a map. But avoiding paths, bandits and an area known for bears added 4K and steep terrain to the route.

Their overnight camp was in dense forest half a kilometre from the heavy fence around Sherwood Castle's private grounds.

A four-person advance party had set up camp days earlier. Three family-sized tents had been erected, each coated with greenery to diffuse heat and prevent detection by patrol drones.

To breach the heavy fence, the advance party had dug a nine-metre tunnel near the castle's hunting grounds, and a back-up in case Castle Guards discovered them.

They were also supposed to set up a satellite connection, enabling the AFM raid to be live-streamed over the internet. But the tunnelling had fallen behind schedule, so Robin and the others arrived to find none of the tech stuff working.

Robin liked messing around with computers and normally would have been happy to set up the remote internet connection, but the sun was low when they finally arrived and all he wanted was to kick off his boots, eat his sandwich and crash out in a corner.

Instead he found himself ten metres up a tree with a head lamp, a tool belt and a coil of rope. After sawing a couple of branches to create a clear line of sight for the dish, Robin lowered the rope. At the bottom, Freya tied on a small satellite transceiver and, once he'd pulled it up,

Robin balanced precariously as he screwed a clamp to a branch and mounted the dish.

It took ten minutes' fiddling with a signal meter to get the dish pointed towards the right satellite and Robin had a painful climb down because his hands were full of splinters.

Most of the AFM activists were vegetarian, so Robin sat in moonlight getting bitten to death by midges, dunking his sandwich in vegan goulash with one hand, while Indio tweezered splinters out of the other.

'Marion thinks she's missing out!' he joked, as she pulled a large splinter that left a trickle of blood down his wrist.

While Robin ate, Freya finished setting up the internet connection and successfully tested live video from one of the helmet cameras.

Robin had left his expensive new laptop back in his den, but he'd put his hacking tools on a memory stick. He needed to make some final checks on Sherwood Castle and yawned as he plugged the USB into a toughened Panasonic laptop and tunnelled into the StayNet system.

Azeem, Lucy and a guy who smelled exactly how you'd expect after four days digging tunnels without a shower formed an audience as Robin logged in and opened the *staff* module.

'I went in here a week ago and changed the shifts for the Castle Guards,' he explained as he ticked a box so that the module showed active security staff on a timeline. 'I thought someone might notice and change it back, but it looks like nobody checks shift rotas after they're entered into the system.'

'What have you changed?' the mud-caked tunneller asked.

Robin scrolled up the screen, showing a grid with lots of red dots.

'The Castle is full of VIP guests ready for tomorrow's trophy hunt. According to the schedule, they should be having welcome drinks in the main ballroom right now. Each of these twenty-nine dots is a guard on duty. The yellow dot means someone called in sick.'

Robin scrolled down to the following day, and a grid with a lot less dots.

'I cancelled a heap of guards on tomorrow's rota. When we enter the castle grounds in the morning, there should only be eleven guards covering the whole compound.

'Why not cancel them all?' the tunneller asked.

'We pulled as many as we dared,' Lucy explained. 'But they'd notice straight away if no guards turned up at all.'

'Eleven of them, fourteen of us,' Robin said, stifling another yawn. 'And we have the element of surprise . . .'

40. OWW, ME LEGS

Sebsebe bet his pals on the Barnsdale rugby squad that he could climb on the roof of the boathouse, make a running leap over the muddy slipway used to launch boats and land in water deep enough not to kill himself.

Since he landed in water and didn't die, he won the bet. But the slipway extended further into the water than the sozzled teen expected and he'd broken his heel and dislocated his shoulder when he slammed concrete beneath a metre of water.

While several onlookers laughed and uploaded the fail to social media, more considerate teens lifted Sebsebe out of the water. One called an ambulance, while another anonymously phoned the school office.

Clare Gisborne hadn't seen the horrifying leap, but after two wrestling bouts and too many beers, she found herself caught in a fleeing mob.

Staff traditionally turned a blind eye to older kids having a little fun after curfew, but that didn't stretch to YouTube videos where the son of Ethiopia's richest businessman hurled himself off the boathouse. Barnsdale had a reputation to protect and there would be consequences for any pupil caught near the scene.

Clare tripped when someone cut across her path. Someone else almost trampled her, but moments later the crowd was gone and she was face down in damp grass, with nothing but moonlight and Sebsebe's distant moans for company. She rolled onto her back and laughed drunkenly as she stared at a swirling grey sky.

Clare knew if she got caught, her dad would probably laugh. *She's a wild one, like her old man!* But that felt wrong; she'd spent years seeking Daddy's approval, but now she'd grown out of it. She remembered her plan to study hard and go to a uni as far from Locksley as she could.

But when Clare tried to get up, her legs were jelly. She felt like crying, laughing and puking all at the same time.

'Look at the state of you!' Little John gasped, arriving on the scene as another of Sebsebe's moans echoed across the rowing lake.

'I've never drunk this much before,' Clare confessed. 'You're a nice guy, coming back for me.'

'I couldn't see you in the pack and I saw how much beer you were necking,' John said, trying not to think about how he'd be most of the way back to school now if he'd legged it with Amber and her pals. 'Put your arms around me.'

Clare managed to sit up as John squatted down to give a piggyback. He still had aches and sunburn from rugby practice and Clare had a hefty frame and muscle from years of kick-boxing.

'You're like concrete,' he moaned, as he started waddling forward.

But John was strong and, once he got going, piggybacking Clare wasn't bad.

After half a kilometre cutting through trees, the school buildings were in sight, but the last stretch to their hall of residence was the most precarious. Crossing the open ground of two sports pitches.

Several of the school's carers, teachers and senior staff were out on the fields. Some of the mob had been caught, while other kids got lucky and made it through.

'We're so busted!' Clare said, her voice jerking to the rhythm of John's huge strides.

Little John dithered before breaking onto the pitches, but he had two advantages. First, he'd drunk less than half a beer, so unlike most kids, he had his wits about him. Second, all the staff he could see were dealing with kids they'd already nabbed. So being among the last to get back had actually worked to their advantage.

'Hang on,' John said. 'It'll get bumpy!'

As Clare pulled her arms too tight for comfort, John broke into a full sprint. He made it across one soccer pitch, but as he reached an all-weather pitch closer to the dorms a man shouted, 'Get 'ere, you little hooligan!'

One of the school grounds-people went wide to intercept, but bottled it when he saw John's bulk charge out of the shadows. John reached the hall of residence seconds later, but the main door didn't budge.

'Around the side!' a boy shouted, gesturing from an upstairs window.

John scrambled around the long building. A couple of kids had opened the windows of their rooms to let escapees climb in, but with Clare in a state John figured it was best to go the extra distance to a side door that someone had propped with a mop.

He had to put her down on the threshold so he didn't whack her head on the door frame. He hoped she'd regained enough coordination for the walk upstairs up to her room, but when he set her feet on the ground, her head rolled and her legs gave way.

'Great,' John groaned, as he caught her.

The dormitory ceiling was too low for another piggyback. Several excitable kids had their heads poking out of their rooms as John grabbed Clare around the waist and threw her over his shoulder.

He got a thigh workout carrying her up to the first floor, and the lad who'd shouted out of the window helped by opening the door of her room.

'She OK?' he asked.

'Yeah,' John said, grunting as he straightened Clare's duvet with his free hand before flopping her onto the bed, unconscious. 'I guess she'll sleep it off.'

41. THE PROBLEM WITH FINGERPRINT LOGINS

Little John rolled Clare onto her front so she couldn't choke, then gently pulled her muddy Nikes off, though he suspected she wouldn't have stirred if he'd set off fireworks. Finally, John crashed into the chair at Clare's desk, catching his breath and realising that he had a shocking pain in his shoulder and skin peeling off his sunburned neck.

The houses at Barnsdale were mixed, but there were strict rules about boys and girls going in each other's rooms, especially after dark and with doors closed.

John wanted to be in his own bed looking innocent if staff came knocking, but as he stood he noticed Clare's phone bulging in the pocket of her shorts. She'd been the closest thing he'd had to a friend since he'd arrived at Barnsdale, but he still wondered if Clare's transformation from ninja-star nutter to vulnerable human was a ploy to get information about Robin.

John felt guilty as he unzipped her pocket and slid out her phone. He'd seen her unlock it with the index finger on her right hand. She was snoring with her fists bunched, but didn't stir as John uncurled the finger and dabbed it on the screen.

Fingerprint Recognised

John studied the icons on Clare's home screen and tapped her messaging app. After glancing to make sure she was still zonked, he opened the conversation between Clare and her dad.

He skimmed through heaps of routine daddy–daughter stuff. School pickups, orthodontist appointments, pleading for money to join Barnsdale's showjumping club, dates for a family party and updates on a great-aunt who tripped on a kerb and broke her arm.

John decided the most likely way to find out whose side Clare was really on was to scroll back to the date when he'd first arrived at Barnsdale. He found a short, upbeat message from Clare to her dad.

I'm alive! Wasn't too much traffic on the highway. Room and teachers seem OK. But guess who I ran into!

In the days that followed, Clare sent messages where she sounded lonely and homesick, but as she'd told John, Guy Gisborne showed little interest in his daughter's welfare and peppered her with excitable and sometimes bizarre suggestions for ways she might get information about Robin out of Little John.

They ranged from flirting and blackmail, to smuggling in wine to get John drunk. John felt offended when Gisborne suggested that Clare try and make friends with John's friends and she'd replied:

Little John's a weirdo, he doesn't have friends.

But mostly he was relieved, because Clare clearly hadn't been spying on him. He even smirked at the irony when he read a message where Gisborne suggested that Clare sneak into his room and try reading the messages on his phone.

John looked up as Clare made a gasping snore, but she showed no sign of waking. It was good knowing Clare had become a true friend. But that also made him feel guiltier about stealing her fingerprint and reading her private information.

As John scrolled back to more recent messages, it seemed that his name had dropped out of the conversation. But as he was about to give up, his eye caught Robin's name in a bout of three-day-old messages.

Clare: Hi-ho daddy-o! Did you pay school for my China trip yet? 20% deposit due Friday.
Daddy: Didn't get chance today. Came out of meeting earlier and found Black Bess II with tyres slashed and Robin Hood Lives graffiti.
Clare: Bummer!

Daddy: People have zero respect now. Your little brothers are teased at school, your ma got donuts flung at her in the street and business is way down. It can't go on, but I'm close to fixing the little brat who set it all off.

Clare: Robin still hiding at Designer Outlets?

Daddy: For sure. That dirty hippy Scarlock has security well organised, but I've found some good people. Former special forces soldiers. They're confident they can put together a snatch squad, overwhelm Scarlock's guards and kidnap Robin.

Clare: What about the Sheriff?

Daddy: Marjorie won't like me making a move for Robin inside Sherwood Forest, but it'll be worth the risk when he tastes my whip!

42. ALL IN THE TIMING

It was just after 8 a.m. Robin had eaten two bananas and a breakfast wrap and now sat on the floor of the tent he'd slept in, pouring paintballs into the gun propped between his legs. He was dressed in camouflage, with goggles and an action camera wrapped around a black combat helmet that was too big for him.

'Sleep OK?' Freya asked, as she stepped inside and squatted on a fold-out stool in front of a pair of toughened laptops.

'I did,' Robin said, as he turned the gas cylinder making his gun hiss. 'Once we got the internet going, I was wiped.'

'Flip your camera on,' Freya said.

Robin reached up to his helmet and tapped a rocker switch. After a couple of seconds, his view appeared in a box on one of the laptop screens.

'Say something,' Freya said.

'Hello. I'm Robin Hood, and I'm about to kick some butt!'

'Sounds good.' Freya gave a thumbs up. 'I'll check Chris and Adrianna's cameras, then your team can ship out.'

'I'll go pee,' Robin said, hanging his paintball gun around his neck and grabbing a backpack that weighed half what it had when he'd left Designer Outlets.

'Catch!' Azeem shouted, when Robin came back from watering a tree.

There was a clanking sound as he plucked a metal cylinder out of the air.

'Smoke grenade,' Azeem explained. 'We've got more than we need. Could make your life easier if you're in the woods trying to get away.'

'Hopefully it won't come to that,' Robin said, as he hooked the grenade to his belt.

Someone's watch bleeped in the background and Lucy took charge, clapping and shouting: 'Team A, it's go time!'

Freya was having a problem with Adrianna's helmet camera and rushed inside to grab a spare. But Lucy stopped her.

'One less camera isn't the end of the world,' she said. 'But our timings are crucial.'

One of the tunnellers handed out walkie-talkies before leading Team A out of the camp. He was followed by Robin, the vets Chris and Adrianna, then sisters Lyla and Azeem looking tough at the rear.

'Keep safe,' Indio told Robin firmly. 'Stick close to Azeem. Her number-one job is to protect you.'

Robin gave Indio a quick hug before scrambling off. It was half a kilometre from camp to the tunnel, and the walk was easy because the tunnellers had trampled the path down over several days.

Robin felt intimidated when the fence around Sherwood Castle's hunting grounds came into view. Ten metres high, with thick concrete posts, it stretched as far as he could see and was clearly designed to keep humans out as much as animals in. The top was barbed wire and the base was set in a deep concrete-filled trench, so you couldn't burrow beneath.

Team A settled in a well-shielded area thirty metres outside the fence, awaiting the signal for their next move. A Castle Guard patrol drone set everyone on edge but zipped over without slowing. Then there was eerie calm as they watched a young deer chewing on shrubs inside the fence.

Nobody spoke, but they all knew if they didn't stop the trophy hunt, there was a chance the deer would get shot by hunters or become lunch for one of the more powerful animals that would be released into the hunting ground to entertain the guests.

The team had been squatting for five minutes when a siren broke in the distance. It had been triggered by an AFM activist crashing a truck into the northernmost section of the hunting ground two kilometres away. The raid organisers hoped some of the depleted security team would be sent to investigate, leaving fewer staff to deal with the real raid.

Robin looked up as another drone skimmed towards the siren, and a minute later they heard engines.

Lucy's voice came over everyone's radio. 'Team Z has breached the fence and sighted security teams on quad bikes. Team A, it's showtime!'

'Copy that, Team A is go!' Azeem told her radio, as she scrambled after the tunneller.

Smashing through the concrete below the fence would have triggered an alarm, so the tunnellers had found a spot hidden by the branches of two large trees. They'd dug two-and-a-half-metres down, then tunnelled nine metres horizontally beneath the fence, exiting with a gentle slope amidst thick shrubs inside the castle grounds.

'Air is pretty foul, so best to take a deep breath and hold it while you're in there,' the tunneller warned.

As Robin clambered down footholds cut into the mud, he realised how tough it must have been for the team to dig the thick clay soil in a few days. While Robin took off his pack, the tunneller used a plastic bowl to bail water that had collected in the bottom overnight. The tunneller then crawled in, unrolling heavy plastic sheeting ahead of himself to save the others from crawling along a muddy floor.

At the far end, the tunneller knocked away branches covering the exit. Azeem went in next, and her shoulders were almost broad enough to touch both sides. Robin slotted his pack into the tunnel mouth and slid it along the plastic in front of himself as he crawled on his belly.

He tried not to breathe, but it was hard work and Lyla dropping her pack in behind shut out all the light. Robin didn't like the dark and took a panicked breath that smelled like mushrooms and made him cough.

The walls and ceiling seemed well braced, but Robin was relieved when the tunneller helped him to his feet and pointed him towards Azeem in a copse a few metres away.

43. SHOOT TO MISS

Sebsebe was in hospital after a flight in an air ambulance and Barnsdale School awoke in uproar. Luckily for Little John, his 07:15 helicopter pickup meant he got away before the headmaster called the whole school into chapel for a dressing down and a lecture on the dangers of alcohol.

Shortly after take-off, he was pleased by a short message from Clare.

My head hurts! Thx for saving me last night!

John had barely slept because he was worried about Robin and he'd crept into Clare's room a couple of times to make sure she was OK.

It was too noisy to use his phone in the chopper, but once John hit the landing pad at Sherwood Castle, he hurried to his room, bolted the door of his en-suite bathroom and called the lawyer, Tybalt Bull.

'You gave me this number when you were helping my dad,' John told Tybalt's voicemail. 'The number I have for Robin is dead, so please call back because I need to get in touch *urgently*. He's in danger, and I know you have ways to contact the leaders at Designer Outlets.'

After leaving the message he rubbed his tired eyes and splashed water on his face.

As he stepped back into his bedroom, he saw a traditional hunter's field suit had been laid out on his bed, complete with baggy plus-four trousers, long socks and a tweed cap. There was also a long walnut box containing a matching shotgun and hunting rifle. John knew nothing about guns, but the beautiful wooden box made him suspect they were expensive.

He hated the idea of hunting and wanted to confront his mum. But John knew he'd get bulldozed and wind up dressed in a silly suit shooting at furry things no matter what he said. So he decided the easiest option was to play along and shoot to miss.

John stepped out of his room and saw that his mum was heading out, but his phone rang before he got a chance to say good morning. It was an unrecognised number, but Tybalt's voice came on the other end.

John didn't go into his friendship with Clare, or how he'd unlocked her phone. He just told Tybalt that Gisborne was hiring a posse of special-forces soldiers to snatch Robin.

'I'll feed your info straight to Will Scarlock,' Tybalt said. 'I'll also put feelers out to see if anyone else has heard anything.'

'Thank you,' John said. 'Gisborne seemed *really* confident that this team could snatch Robin from the mall. What do you think Scarlock will do?'

'My expertise is in the courtroom not the forest,' Tybalt said. 'But Scarlock is crafty. I'm sure he'll take the threat seriously and find a way to keep Robin safe.'

'I hope so,' John said. 'Me and my brother have our differences, but that doesn't mean I want Gisborne getting hold of him.'

'And your father cares deeply for both of you,' Tybalt stressed. 'He's worried about Robin's situation.'

'Have you seen my dad since he was sentenced?' John asked.

'I have many clients in the Pelican Island prison complex. If I have time, I visit your father when I'm over there.'

'How's he doing?'

'The bikers are making sure Ardagh is well looked after and protected from any friends of Gisborne. Obviously it's impossible for Robin to visit, but your father is sad that you haven't seen him.'

'My mum says her assistant filled out an application but they haven't approved my visitor status yet.'

Tybalt coughed awkwardly. 'I hate to call your mother a liar, but there's no approval process for close family. You can book an inmate visit through the Pelican Island website.'

John tutted and shook his head. 'I'll nag Mum again. If you see my dad, tell him I love him.'

'I'll do that, and I'll contact Will Scarlock immediately,' Tybalt said. 'Enjoy your weekend.'

'Thanks,' John said. Then, after Tybalt hung up, 'I certainly won't.'

44. HUNTING FOR DUMMIES

While hunters in natural settings trek through kilometres of difficult terrain and often spend days tracking large prey, Sherwood Castle's carefully designed acreage was more like a hunters' theme park. The trees were spread out and the undergrowth closely cropped so that animals couldn't hide, while neat bark-covered paths were wide enough for hunters to shoot from the comfort of an SUV.

'Are we sure there's nothing out here that'll eat us?' Robin asked warily, as Team A dashed between trees, dodging open ground populated with deer.

Adrianna answered. 'Exotic animals get shipped in for trophy hunts and cost a heap of money. Sheriff Marjorie won't have them roaming around eating King Corporation's deer, unless someone is paying to hunt them.'

'Makes sense,' Robin said, but kept glancing around suspiciously. 'Is it true you worked here?'

Adrianna nodded and pointed to the other vet. 'Chris and I both did work experience when we were training.'

'We said one day we'd do something about the trophy hunts,' Chris added, as he smiled at Adrianna. 'And here we are.'

Team A had been jogging inside the fence for a kilometre when they came to the southern edge where the hunting ground met the castle resort. There was a corrugated metal building, sixty metres long, with giant slow-turning ventilation fans at each end.

As Robin got close, he caught animal sounds and a funk of manure.

'Helmet cams on,' Azeem said.

Freya's voice came over the walkie-talkie. 'I have strong signals on all cameras. Lyla, you have a dead bug on your lens.'

As Lyla wiped the camera strapped to her helmet, the young vets and a few others who didn't want be identified pulled on balaclavas and Azeem tried the metal door at the back of the shed. When it didn't open, she banged on the metal and waited.

'Nobody home,' Azeem said.

But as she reached for a crowbar to break the lock, a worker in wellies and filthy blue overalls leaned out and looked startled when he saw the five members of Team A.

'What in the –'

Before another word came out, Lyla grabbed him around the neck and nipped him with a stun gun on its lowest setting.

'Who else is in there?' Azeem demanded, wrenching the worker's arm behind his back and dropping him to his knees.

'Just me.'

'What about the office?' Adrianna asked.

'A young lass. A student.'

'Call her,' Azeem demanded.

'No funny business,' Lyla added, as she brandished the stun gun. 'Unless you want a taste of this on the high setting.'

'Xolani,' he shouted.

Robin dry-heaved at the stench of urine and manure coming out of the door as they backed out of sight.

Xolani was a small, stocky teen and Azeem watched through a ventilation shaft as she approached the end of the shed and spoke suspiciously.

'Gene, what's up? Who's out there with you?'

Robin tried to figure how Xolani had spotted them and guessed she'd seen shadows shifting through vents in the shed walls.

'Everything's fine,' Gene said. 'Just some questions about the schedule for the hunt.'

Xolani must have sensed nerves in Gene's voice, because she spun around and started running.

Azeem and Lyla charged in after her. The shed had animal pens and barred cages on either side, tightly packed with big cats, zebras, bears and ostriches, while the central channel between them was thick with straw and muck.

Xolani was speedy, but Azeem caught her up as she fumbled to open the door at the opposite end.

'We're not hurting you!' Azeem said. 'Just shut up and let us do our job.'

Xolani grabbed the door handle and tried to wriggle out, but Azeem swung her around into the bars of a cage and Lyla closed in with the stun gun.

'Who are you?' Xolani spat furiously, as she raised her hands.

'Animal Freedom Militia,' Lyla said proudly.

'Turn around, put your hands behind your back,' Azeem demanded.

As Lyla looped plastic handcuffs through a barred gate then locked them on Xolani's wrists, Chris marched Gene back inside and did the same.

'Stand still and mouths shut,' Azeem said. 'This will be over in minutes and you won't get hurt unless you give us a reason.'

45. WHEN MUM PICKS YOUR CLOTHES

Little John's size meant he got stares wherever he went. Wearing baggy trousers tucked into long socks, plus a tweed jacket and matching deerstalker made him feel like Sherlock Holmes in a school play as he rode down in the penthouse's polished brass lift.

Soft-spoken waiters bowed as he entered Sherwood Castle's Dome restaurant.

'Good morning, Mr Kovacevic. Your mother has a seat for you at her table.'

The Dome usually served a generous breakfast buffet to golfers, wedding guests and conference attendees, but on this Saturday regular guests had to eat in a windowless conference room, while this glass-domed space was cordoned off for elite trophy hunters.

Piped classical music had been replaced with a live string quartet, the buffet's bacon and hash browns swapped for ice sculptures and, instead of grabbing your own plate, bow-tied waiters delivered platters to tables and eagerly refilled glasses from giant jeroboams of champagne.

John felt less awkward when he realised most guests were in traditional hunting gear similar to his own, but that only lasted until he dopily bumped into Lucasta Twist, the pop princess whose hit song had everyone bopping at his primary-school leavers disco.

'Sorry,' John said, starstruck.

Lucasta hadn't made a hit in five years, but the diamond on her wedding ring was the size of a grape.

The famous and beautiful had been given the most visible tables, while Little John found his mother with two overweight men in a discreet booth off to one side. Their table bore enough fancy food platters to eat for a week, and John noticed that the champagne on this table was in tatty regular-sized bottles, that he suspected were very old and far more expensive that what everyone else was quaffing.

'At last, we meet the long-lost son!' one of the men said, as he pulled up his bulging frame to shake hands.

'John, this is Richard King III,' Marjorie said proudly.

John shook hands with the jovial Richard King, then his brother John King, who was much younger. His huge eyebrows and dark hunting tartan gave him a vampire-like air.

Little John had seen the billionaire brothers in news stories, from the owners' box at Macondo United matches to shifty appearances in front of government committees investigating riots at their network of private prisons. Ardagh often went into a rant and called the King brothers crooks when their names came up, and John felt uneasy having them sat across the breakfast table.

'Pleasure to meet, young man,' John King said, raising one of his caterpillar-sized eyebrows.

'My mum talks about you all the time,' Little John told Richard.

Richard laughed. 'Good things, I hope.'

'Always,' Marjorie grovelled to Richard. 'You're my mentor, and a true friend.'

Marjorie's anxiety was noticeable because it was the first time Little John had seen his mother in a situation where she wasn't bossing people around.

Little John's words dried up after the handshakes, so he grabbed an empty plate and began scoffing meat sliced so thin it was transparent.

'You have a great turnout this year,' Richard King told Marjorie, as a waiter filled Little John's glass with mineral water and offered him a menu.

'Just bring another bottle of the '85 Moët and platter of the good sashimi!' Marjorie ordered. 'And more carpaccio – my boy seems to be enjoying that.'

46. NOT SO FRESH IN HERE

Robin was the last member of Team A to enter Sherwood Castle's animal shed. Sheila's chicken coops could get fragrant on a warm morning, but the stench and heat of two hundred large animals crammed into the gloomy shed was like the Locksley High boys' toilets times a billion.

The two vets unzipped their backpacks and began pulling out ziplock bags filled with scraps of meat, sugar cubes and grain.

'Lyla, keep lookout,' Azeem ordered.

Robin wished he was the one getting out of whatever nastiness was squelching under his boots. Instead he got handed a video camera fitted with a rectangular panel light to point at the two masked vets.

'This dingy shed is where exotic animals are kept before hunts at Sherwood Castle,' Adrianna began, doing her best impression of a newsreader as zebras brayed and backed away from the light. 'Not only are animals here crammed into cages too small for their needs, ruminants like the zebras behind me are housed close to predators, leaving them in a state of constant agitation and terror.'

Chris took over the talk to camera. 'In a few hours, the Sheriff of Nottingham's staff plan to hose the filth off these beautiful creatures, then release them into the castle hunting grounds to be killed for the enjoyment of wealthy, sadistic hunters.'

'Sadly, it isn't safe to set these animals free so far from their native environments,' Adrianna said. 'But we've brought some of their favourite treats and laced them with a harmless tranquilliser. This will send them to sleep for several hours and make them useless for today's hunt.

'But this is a temporary solution. It's up to you, the viewer of this video, to ensure that these animals are given decent new homes. Please help the AFM campaign by emailing Sheriff Marjorie's party, to say that you won't vote for a candidate who supports trophy hunting in the upcoming elections. And boycott all King Corporation products and services until the Sherwood Castle hunting grounds are permanently closed.'

Chris handed Robin a bag of tranquilliser-laced sugar lumps. Adrianna filmed as Robin placed a few in his palm and warily allowed ostriches to peck them out of his hand.

While the camera operator shot carefully framed video of Robin feeding apple chunks to zebras and diced lamb to leopards, Lyra, Adrianna and Chris worked rapidly, making sure plenty of tranquillised treats got thrown into every cage.

Once the food was distributed, Azeem radioed through to Lucy. 'Team A reporting in. Phase one is complete with no major issues.'

'Great to hear,' Lucy called back. 'Team B is in position. Lyla to liaise up top, the rest of you head down to meet Team B at the exit point.'

'Copy that, boss,' Azeem said. 'Over and out.'

Exiting the animal shed at the opposite end to where they'd entered took the team beyond the hunting grounds, into a zone behind Sherwood Castle full of storage sheds, a laundry with steam rising from a chimney and parking for utility vehicles such as tractors and forklifts. It was screened by a tree-lined embankment, so no resort guest would ever see it.

'Be safe up there!' Azeem told Lyla, as the sisters bumped fists.

As Lyla headed right and began scrambling up the embankment, Robin, Azeem and the two vets went left.

'Feeling OK?' Azeem asked Robin as they walked briskly.

'So far, so good,' Robin said cheerfully, before looking down at his feet. 'Except my boots smell like animal butt.'

Azeem laughed as she glanced at her watch. 'Look on the bright side – in a few minutes we get to shoot paintballs at idiots.'

47. THIS ZEBRA SO YUMMY

'Are you interested in business?' John King asked.

Little John realised he was being spoken to, but had his chops stuffed with meat.

'I guess,' John said, as he swallowed too fast. 'As much as anyone.'

John King seemed unimpressed with the lukewarm answer. 'Looking around this room can teach you a lot about how to make connections with powerful people,' he explained. 'These folks can buy whatever they want. Tailored clothes, handmade watches, houses, even aeroplanes. But they can't buy Sheriff Marjorie's legendary trophy hunt. Everyone wants to be your mother's best friend, just to get an invite.'

'Genius,' Richard King agreed, as he gobbled chunks of tuna belly. 'That word is bandied about everywhere, but I identified your mother's potential when she was a twenty-two-year-old running a dozen branches of Captain Cash.'

'But what about the hunting?' Little John asked, as his mother smiled at the compliments. 'Surely not everyone's idea of fun?'

For a second he thought his mum might be annoyed by this comment, but she nodded thoughtfully.

'It's not for everyone,' Marjorie agreed. 'But the ones who come like the fact that they're going deep into the forest, to get spoiled with food and booze and do something that's thrilling and a little bit bad.'

'Hunting is as natural as farting,' John King said airily, as he necked vintage champagne. 'It's human nature to enjoy a conquest over an animal.'

Richard King cupped one hand over his mouth and whispered in Little John's ear. 'And sure, the hunters get to eat and shoot for free, but we make our money back when they hit the casino afterwards!'

As John smiled awkwardly, the waiter set another meat platter on the table, then pointed out the four different types.

'On our exotic carpaccio platter, you have a selection of zebra, rhinoceros, bison and kangaroo.'

John's draw dropped. 'Wait . . . What's carpaccio?'

The waiter smiled politely. 'Carpaccio is raw meat, sliced wafer thin.'

John hacked a mouthful into his napkin and blurted. 'Did I just eat half a raw zebra?'

The King brothers found this hilarious, but Marjorie was horrified.

'Don't spit in your napkin!' she barked. 'Show some manners!'

John felt humiliated and his anger at his mother welled up.

He wanted to tell her that he didn't want to wear a stupid hunting suit and go out with a bunch of rich idiots killing defenceless animals. He wanted his mum to stop making excuses that stopped him from visiting his dad in prison, and he wanted her to accept that his name was John Hood, not Kovacevic.

The string quartet abruptly stopped playing Mozart, and Little John was so wrapped in angry thoughts that for an instant he imagined he'd become so red in the face that the whole room was staring at him. But his mother saw something else and shot up from her seat, and there were screams as pieces of glass crashed onto tables from the dome above.

John tracked the falling shards, then looked up further and saw two silhouetted figures, dressed in combat gear and clambering over the outside of the glass dome.

Marjorie yelled into a walkie-talkie. 'Moshe, why do we have broken glass and two women crawling around on the dome above my pre-hunt banquet?'

Moshe came back fast and breathless. 'Sheriff, I just heard. I'm sending someone across to see what's going on.'

'I don't need to be told what's going on!' Marjorie roared. 'I'm looking right at it, and I need you to deal with it.'

Up above, a *Stop Trophy Hunting* pennant unfurled through the broken dome and a young woman shouted, 'Murderers. You should all be ashamed of yourselves!'

'I'm on my way,' Moshe told Marjorie. 'But I'm right out at the north end of the hunting ground. Someone crashed a van into the fence. When we approached, a booby trap went off and drenched us in red paint.'

'Where's everyone else?' Marjorie asked.

'We are the Animal Freedom Militia!' one of the ninjas on the roof shouted through the dome. 'Consider this your final warning.'

'There was some mix-up with the shifts,' Moshe said. 'We're ridiculously short-staffed.'

John tried to hide a smirk – his mother looked as if she was about to crush her walkie-talkie like a tin can. But his smile didn't last, because the activists had begun lobbing bright red smoke bombs through the hole in the dome.

48. SHOOTING RICH IN A BARREL

Robin could see Freya and Lyla pulling pins out of smoke bombs and lobbing them through the glass dome as he lay face down on a neat lawn, fifty metres away. They'd met with Indio, Lucy and the other three members of Team B, and had paintball guns at the ready.

As the build-up of red smoke made a chimney out of the hole in the dome, Lucy used a phone to upload a photo of the wretched conditions inside the animal shed on the AFM social media, accompanied by a short message.

```
See justice for these animals in 5...
4...3...2...1...
#Livestream
#AFM
#Animal rights
```

As smoke built inside the dome, the wealthy guests began a panicked exit through doors leading onto a white stone patio.

'That's what's-his-name,' Azeem said, pointing to a hunky man holding a napkin over his mouth and coughing. 'Married to the actress with all the teeth.'

'Wait until there are more people out there,' Indio said firmly. 'And remember, avoid shooting staff, and no shots above chest height.'

'Richard King and Sheriff Marjorie!' Robin whispered to Azeem. Then felt less sure of himself as another figure ran out. 'And . . . my brother.'

Indio stood up and gave the signal. 'Let's shoot 'em all!'

Robin sprang up and bolted, but Azeem yanked him back. 'You stick close to me!'

Smoke was billowing out of the open patio doors as Freya and Lyla slid off the dome.

Robin and the others charged past a bewildered elderly couple taking a jog on one of the castle paths. The videographer and a battery of helmet cameras filmed every shot as nine paintball guns opened up on the patio.

'Murderers!' Lucy shouted.

Robin and Azeem dropped into firing positions and let rip. The King brothers and Sheriff Marjorie were a popular target. But so many people were going after them, Robin decided it was his mission to stop anyone from getting off the patio unscathed.

He was frustrated by waiting staff getting in the way, but he spotted a couple jumping down onto a gravel path. He shot the man between shoulder blades with two big red splats, then targeted tartan hunting trousers stretched over a woman's arse.

He hit the back of her thigh, making the running woman trip over her own leg and lurch sideways into a holly bush. As her partner shielded his face and tried to yank her out of the prickly leaves, Robin blasted more paintballs at her flailing legs.

'This is fun!' Robin whooped to Azeem. 'I hope my camera's getting all this!'

The smoke pouring out of the restaurant made things hazy as Azeem splattered the last few guests coming through the doors. Robin fired at a man jumping off the patio, but stopped when he realised he was carrying a crying toddler dressed in a mini tartan hunting suit.

'Dammit!' Azeem shouted urgently.

'What?' Robin asked, as he realised his gun was out of ammo.

'The girls,' Azeem said, pointing. 'Freya looks hurt.'

Robin squinted into the smoke. Guests and staff had now cleared the dome exits, but Freya had turned her ankle when she jumped from the base of the dome onto a lawn beside the patio. She was bigger than Lyla, so Lyla was struggling to get her up.

'I've got to help my sister,' Azeem said, pointing away to one side. 'Indio and Chris are over there, stick with them.'

'You go,' Robin agreed. 'I don't need babysitting.'

Dense red smoke faded to pink as the first wafts reached Robin's position. While Azeem sprinted fearlessly through flying paintballs towards the patio, Robin thought about running straight across to Indio. But he'd already opened his bag to load a new paintball-filled hopper.

Lucy's triumphant voice came over his radio. 'We've done what we came for, folks. Let's leave before the Castle Guards get organised!'

Part of the withdrawal plan was to leave behind a curtain of smoke bombs, making it harder for anyone to chase as the activists climbed back into the hunting grounds and sprinted to their tunnel.

Unfortunately, this meant Robin was down on one knee, attaching his paintball-filled hopper as several of his comrades set off large smoke cannisters. By the time he stood, the smoke was so thick that everything below his waist was in a haze and he wasn't sure which way he was facing.

'Where the hell have you been!' he heard Sheriff Marjorie shout in the distance. 'Spread out. Launch the drones. I want every one of those scumbags in my cells!'

The smoke kept getting thicker. Robin was sure the Sheriff's voice had come from his right, and he caught a break as a gap in the smoke gave him a clear view of the glass dome.

'Thank God,' he said to himself, as he turned and started a brisk walk away.

Once he'd covered a hundred metres, the smoke was thin enough that Robin felt he could run without tripping on a kerb or smashing head first into a tree. As he sprinted towards the hunting grounds, he heard quad-bike engines somewhere behind.

He had to get back inside the hunting grounds to reach the tunnel. They'd arrived at the castle via the animal shed, but the two handcuffed workers would almost certainly have been discovered, so going back the same way was too risky.

The fence where the hunting grounds met the castle was nothing like the elaborate one bordering open forest. The three metres of wire was only designed to keep animals in and could be climbed by any reasonably fit person.

As Robin got close, he saw Indio and a couple of the others scrambling over. He thought about shouting at them to wait, but figured he'd soon catch up. A drone skimmed overhead and the quad bikes were getting louder, but Robin didn't realise how close they were until a quad burst out of haze less than thirty metres to his right.

He dived forward and glanced over his shoulder as he frantically crawled towards a raised mound. It had a hexagonal wooden gazebo at the centre, positioned so that hotel guests could sit inside watching red deer in the hunting grounds.

Robin was a few metres from cover when he saw a huge figure cutting between two trees to his left. He rolled onto his belly and aimed his paintball gun as the man closed in, but he only shot branches.

The man was crazy fast, and before Robin knew it a hand grabbed the top of his pack. He got throttled by the strap of his paintball gun as he was dragged gasping along the ground. Then the guy plucked Robin up, carrying him like a shopping bag.

'Help!' Robin shouted. He was facing the ground and all he could see was his captor's huge brown boots, misted with red paint. He'd only ever known one person with feet so stupidly huge . . .

'Keep quiet,' Little John ordered, catching his breath as he took two steps up into the hexagonal gazebo and dumped his little brother on the wooden deck.

49. BROTHERLY LOVE

Robin blinked as he rolled onto his back, hitting the gazebo's wooden bench seat. He was out of breath and his eyes stung from the smoke, but he definitely wasn't hallucinating.

'You reek,' John complained, as he ripped the camera from Robin's helmet and stamped it under his boot. 'Don't people wash in the forest?'

'It's not me, it's from your mummy's disgusting animal shed,' Robin said. 'And sorry if I spoiled your plans. Were you gonna shoot the legs off a couple of ostriches? Maybe put a cap in that cute baby bear I saw?'

'Don't be a dick,' John said, as he let Robin sit up. 'And don't try anything.'

A couple of quad bikes buzzed close to the fence and Robin wondered if he'd have made it over before they grabbed him.

'Are you gonna hand me in?' Robin asked warily, as he counted five red splats on John's clothes.

John looked annoyed and held up his hands. 'What have I ever done, except try to find a way to keep you safe?'

Robin was impressed by Little John's firmness. The big brother he'd grown up with could spend ten minutes deciding which shirt to wear, but the last few months had clearly toughened him up.

'For your information, I was on the phone to Tybalt this morning, trying to save you,' John continued. 'Gisborne's sending a posse out to Designer Outlets. They're total hard cases. Former special forces.'

Robin shook his head. 'Gisborne wouldn't dare. Last time he sent people into the forest, his offices and half of Locksley got trashed in a riot.'

'They're not Gisborne's people,' John said. 'It's a snatch squad. In and out before anyone notices.'

Robin sighed and flicked sweaty hair off his brow. 'Is Tybalt going to tell Will Scarlock?'

'Obviously.' John moved to the edge of the gazebo and glanced about. 'Not that it matters if you get busted here.'

The quad bikes sounded further off than they'd been a minute earlier, but several buzzed like distant flies and the smoke was clearing rapidly.

'I *have* to go,' Robin said. 'The longer I'm here, the less chance I have of making it across the hunting grounds before the guards find our tunnel.'

John nodded. 'How far north?'

'Four minutes if I run flat out.'

'There's a better way,' John said.

But before he could explain, he spotted three women. Two walking as fast as they could, while the third was draped over their shoulders with her boots dangling.

'Looks like your AFM pals,' John said.

Robin shot up and recognised Azeem and Lyla. Freya was the one dangling, with her face screwed up in pain.

'Let me go with them,' Robin pleaded.

John looked wary. 'I guess. But they're hardly gonna sprint, and there's a lot of guards coming up from their quarters in the basement.'

The three women had now reached the fence. Lyla and Azeem could have clambered over in seconds, but Freya's injury was a big problem.

'Hug?' Robin said.

Little John dabbed a tear out of his eye as he gave Robin a quick hug.

'You've always had a taste for danger,' John said. 'Don't let it kill you.'

'I'll do my best,' Robin said.

But as he put his boot on the first step down from the gazebo, he realised the quad bikes were getting loud again. Lyla had scrambled up and sat astride the top of the fence, but Freya needed a boost so Azeem was trying to get her to stand on her shoulders.

But Freya was heavy, and as Azeem struggled to stand, Robin saw the quad skimming in front of the fence and closing fast. Even if he could persuade Little John to step into the open and help Freya over the fence, it would never happen before the quad arrived.

'What are you doing?' Little John asked, as Robin set down the paintball gun hung around his neck and slid his backpack down his arms.

'We're past time for toys,' Robin said, as he ripped out his bow.

50. UNLEASH THY WEAPON OF DOOM

Robin had wrapped his bow in plastic so that it didn't get muddy in the tunnel, and it took several fiddly seconds to undo tape and strip it all away.

Lyla could have run, but loyally jumped back down on the castle side of the fence when she saw the quad. Azeem threw Freya over her shoulder and tried to move, but a second quad sweeping in from the right cut them off.

'Hands up, forest scum!' a Castle Guard in combat gear said, as he switched off his quad and swung a rifle strapped to his back around his head.

Robin stared down his arrow sight as a second guard closed in. His weapon had a huge muzzle with an opening big enough for a man's fist.

'Do you know what that is?' Robin asked.

'It fires balls of sticky grey gloop,' John said. 'I got hit with one when the Castle Guards extracted me from the forest. They won't kill you, but they hurt like hell, and they'll break bones.'

Robin watched as the guards closed on the three women. Lyla and Azeem knelt, but Freya stayed slumped in the grass.

'Are you deaf!' the one with the gloop gun boomed, as he jabbed Freya with the toe of his boot.

'This is all being live-streamed,' Azeem shouted, tapping her helmet camera. 'Castle Guards have no police powers. We demand you release us or take us to the Forest Ranger station.'

'Knees!' gloop gun ordered again.

This time, the other man yanked Freya up. Robin and Little John winced as she screamed in pain.

'She's got a broken ankle,' Lyla shouted.

'You'll have a broken head if you don't shut your yap!' the guard with the gun said.

'I've got a card,' Little John told Robin quietly.

Robin was trying to pick a moment when he could shoot two guards without his comrades getting hurt and was irritated that Little John broke his concentration.

'What are you on about?'

'I have full access,' Little John explained, as he pointed right. 'Even if you shoot both guards and get your injured pal over that fence, she'll be slow. But if you ride those quads out past the animal shed, there's an access gate Castle Guards use when they go into the forest on horseback.'

'Really?' Robin sounded doubtful.

'Take it,' John said, as he took the card out of his ridiculous trousers.

'There'll be a security log,' Robin said. 'They'll know it's your card.'

'I'll say I lost it in the chaos.'

'Will they believe you?'

John shrugged. 'I guess that's my problem.'

Robin smiled awkwardly as he pocketed the white plastic card and looked back at his target.

Out by the fence, the guy with the rifle stood directly in front of the three young women, while the other one had now forced Freya to kneel, stretching her broken ankle into an excruciatingly painful position. He'd set the clumsy gloop gun in the grass and was patting Azeem down, stripping her stun gun and the big machete on her belt.

'I can't stay like this,' Freya begged, as tears streaked down red cheeks. 'My foot is twisted. I'm going to pass out.'

'See if I care!' the guard said cruelly.

As he moved across to search Lyla, Freya groaned and toppled sideways. Azeem instinctively reached out to grab her friend.

The guard with the gun shouted, 'Leave her!' and moved like he was about to shoot Azeem in the head.

It was probably an empty threat, but everyone was moving at once and Robin knew he wouldn't get a better chance. He shot his first arrow, spearing the shoulder of the guard with the gun.

Azeem had good fighting skills and sprang into action, thrusting a palm under the guard's chin that made his head snap backwards.

As she grabbed the rifle, Robin took aim at the other guard. But he didn't have a clear shot because Lyla had jumped up and lunged for the gloop gun. She snatched it out of the grass, swung it around and shot the guard in the belly.

The guard was wearing body armour, but from point-blank range the exploding grey putty lifted him off the ground and doubled him up. Lyla barged him down then stood over him, reloaded and shot him again.

'Take some of what you dish out,' Lyla spat furiously. 'Pig!'

Azeem stood with the gun, looking around while keeping a wary eye on the floored Castle Guards. She could hear more quad bikes and she only knew one person who used a bow, but hadn't seen exactly where Robin's arrow came from.

Back in the gazebo, Robin looked around at Little John. 'I'm only little. We could probably squeeze three on a quad bike if you want to get out of here.'

'Sherwood's all dirt, bugs and crazy kidnappers,' Little John said, looking horrified. 'I'm more use on the inside and I'll just have to put up with living in five-star luxury.'

'Good to finally know whose side you're on,' Robin said, as tears welled in his eyes.

John didn't answer because he was welling up too.

'Give Dad my love when you see him,' Robin said, as he swung his bow over his shoulder and decided he couldn't be bothered to carry the paintball gun any further.

He checked there were no more guards closing in and ran out towards the three women.

'Robin, thank God!' Azeem said. 'Nice shooting, but have you been crying?'

'It's the smoke,' Robin lied.

'Will would have gone *crazy* if he found out that I abandoned you,' Azeem said, as she eyed Freya and the fence warily.

'I won't grass you up if you're really nice to me,' Robin said cheekily, then pointed towards the animal shed. 'We can use the two quads. I have a swipe card that'll unlock the side gate.'

'Whatever we're doing, it needs to be quick,' Lyla said, as she held up a radio she'd ripped off one of the injured guards. 'The drones spotted us and back-up is on the way.'

51. GOT RED ON HER EVERYTHING

Sheriff Marjorie stood in the main hallway of her castle penthouse, wiping a mist of red paint from her brow with a damp towel. Moshe Klein had changed his own trashed suit for a baggy sweatshirt and had never seen his boss angrier.

'You're my head of security,' she roared furiously. 'So please, pretty please, tell me how we only have eleven guards on duty for the biggest event of the year?'

'This has never happened before,' Moshe said, drawing on army-officer training to look strong, while suspecting that he'd be out of a job whatever he said. 'As soon as I arrived, I started looking into it. The log says the shift patterns were altered by Nadine in the IT department.'

'Why can someone I've never heard of in the IT department alter shift patterns?' Marjorie barked, as she threw down the towel and started unbuttoning her paint-splattered hunting jacket.

'IT needs to access all StayNet modules so they can investigate faults,' Moshe explained. 'I got into work at seven this morning and started calling in extra staff as soon as I saw we were short-handed. But I only made three calls before the emergency siren went off.'

'I've been utterly humiliated,' Marjorie roared, as she threw her jacket down. 'Richard and John King have taken their helicopter back to the capital. But quite a few of the other guests are still on site, so I think the best strategy is business as normal. The hunt was due to start at nine, but if we shift it up to –'

'Sheriff,' Moshe interrupted, clearing his throat awkwardly, 'I thought you'd been told. The AFM drugged all the exotics in the shed. They're zonked out, probably for eight to twelve hours. There's absolutely no way we can hunt today.'

Marjorie hissed and stared at a large vase. She imagined hurling it at a wall, but then remembered that it had cost more than a family car and stomped the stained towel instead.

'This is going to cost us millions!' Marjorie said. 'People come here for a relaxing five-star experience. But from now on, when Sherwood Castle is mentioned, all everyone will think of is a shed full of grubby animals, Lucasta Twist falling on her arse under a hail of paintballs and Robin Hood flipping his middle finger at my security camera as he escapes on a stolen quad bike! I'll never –'

Marjorie's flow was interrupted by the doorbell.

'The damage to my reputation could take years to repair. And as for my chances in national politics . . .'

The bell rang again.

'Whoever it is, tell them I'm busy!' the Sheriff shouted to the maid who'd come out of a bathroom to answer the door.

'It's your son, Miss Sheriff,' the maid said nervously.

'Let him in!' Marjorie yelled. 'Why am I surrounded by idiots?'

She felt a rare twinge of motherly instinct when she saw Little John covered in paintball splats and his hair all mussed.

'Sweetheart, are you OK?'

'Few bruises where I got paintballed,' John said. 'I've had worse in rugby training. I rang the bell because I've lost my pass. It must have fell out while I was running in these baggy trousers.'

'Moshe, get him a new pass,' Marjorie said.

Moshe audibly gasped, because getting Little John's pass meant he wasn't being fired. At least not immediately . . .

'Go take a hot shower,' Marjorie told her son. 'And try not to worry. The Sheriff of Nottingham has taken bigger hits than this and come out on top!'

John started unbuttoning his shirt as he walked to his room, but he noticed his mother staring open-mouthed at Moshe, like she was about to say something she didn't want him to hear. So instead of going straight to his shower, John stood just inside his bedroom door. Fortunately, the hard surfaces of the stone hallway carried his mother's voice.

'I'll need to get Darcy from my political office up here so we can put together a damage-limitation strategy,' Marjorie told Moshe. 'But first I have to talk to my old friend.'

'Gisborne?' Moshe guessed.

'Who else?' Marjorie said. 'Give me your phone. I can't have any record showing that I've spoken to him.'

John heard the maid wheeling her cleaning cart into another room. Then his mother talking to Gisborne.

'I'll come right out and say it, Guy,' Marjorie began. 'You were right, I was wrong.'

John could only guess what Gisborne was saying on the other end.

'Guy, I'm sure you and your homeboys are having a time watching me get hit by paintballs on national news, and I know you enjoy needling me, but I have a dozen fires to put out, so can we skip your hilarious banter?'

There was a pause while Gisborne said something.

'Robin Hood was your problem while he was causing havoc in Locksley. But he becomes mine when he hooks up with animal-rights nutters and trashes my hunt. My sources tell me you're putting together a snatch squad to get hold of him.'

After a pause Marjorie broke into a noisy laugh.

'Guy, I know that, because there are so many sneaks and spies in your grubby little organisation I could probably tell you when you last clipped your toenails. My point is this: the posse you're sending to capture Robin Hood now has my full support.

'Anything you need: drone surveillance, tracked vehicles, weapons, horses . . . Your men can use the castle as a base and even have Castle Guard back-up if you want it. Just call Moshe and tell him what you need. And now I'm hanging up.'

Marjorie handed Moshe's phone back, then grabbed the vase and decided that the morning's events deserved twenty thousand pounds' worth of satisfaction.

'Robin Hood,' Sheriff Marjorie screamed. 'I hope he rots!'

The vase crashed into the wall and Moshe shielded his eyes as shards flew in every direction.

BREAKING NEWS

'Good afternoon. I'm Lynn Hoapili with this special update, live from the gates of Sherwood Castle.

'Shortly before nine this morning, a group of Animal Freedom Militia activists, including Robin Hood, stormed Sherwood Castle in an attempt to disrupt Sheriff Marjorie Kovacevic's annual trophy hunt.

'In sensational scenes, which were live-streamed by the group, celebrities including pop diva Lucasta Twist, actor Scott Okoye and TV chef Nick Cobb faced smoke grenades and a barrage of paintballs.

'Over a million social-media users have condemned celebrities and businesspeople for taking part in the hunt. There have also been calls to boycott King Corporation products and the new season of Okoye's hit show, *Star Command*.

'Also trending is dramatic leaked CCTV footage of Robin Hood and three accomplices escaping the castle compound on quad bikes. But in a written statement the Sheriff of Nottingham's office has condemned the attack.'

Text scrolled on screen, as Lynn read it out:

'The Sherwood Trophy Hunt is an annual event that has raised more than £4 million for children's charities. All animals at Sherwood Castle are supervised by trained staff and kept in state-of-the-art conditions. The footage of animal cages released by the AFM was not filmed within castle grounds and should be considered 100% fake news.'

52. EVERYONE WANTS TO BE ROBIN HOOD (EXCEPT ROBIN HOOD)

It was a tough walk back to the mall. The quad bikes were useless in dense forest, so Robin carried as much gear as he could, while Lyla and Azeem hauled Freya the twelve kilometres over tough ground.

Robin wanted to chill in his den once he'd showered away the grime and eaten a late lunch, but Sam Scarlock told him it was no longer safe and a couple of mall guards carried his bedding to a little rest area at the back of Will's command tent.

Robin was tired, but the roof was too hot and noisy to doze, so he played with his laptop, watching all the videos and social-media stuff about the raid.

It ranged from a hilarious slow-motion GIF showing Lucasta Twist's expression as she got hit in the chest with a paintball, to articles claiming that Sheriff Marjorie was a national treasure and Robin Hood was a child being manipulated by evil terrorists.

Robin was proud that he'd become a hero to the kind of folks that people like Guy Gisborne and Sheriff Marjorie liked to dump all over, but it was also overwhelming; he wished it was something he could turn off and go back to being an ordinary kid for a couple of weeks.

'I see the crazy posse hasn't delivered you to Gisborne yet,' Marion said cheerfully, as she walked in, holding Robin's boots by the laces.

The outsides had been thoroughly scrubbed and the laces loosened so the insides could dry out after being nuked with deodorant.

'You cleaned them?' Robin said, surprised.

'The heck I did,' Marion said, disgusted at the thought. 'Aunt Lucy took everyone's boots and scrubbed them with disinfectant. They're still damp, so she says you should leave them in the sun for a bit.'

'Have you seen Freya?'

Marion nodded. 'She's not great. We don't have an X-ray machine, but Dr Gladys thinks it's a complicated break that'll need surgery. They'll have to use a fake ID and try getting treatment in a government hospital. Somewhere far away, because they'll be on the lookout for a girl with a broken ankle in Locksley.'

'That's rough,' Robin said.

'Are you bricking yourself?' Marion asked bluntly.

'About the posse?'

Marion nodded. 'What else?'

'What's to be scared of?' Robin said breezily. 'It's just heavily armed, expertly trained soldiers who want to drag me out of my bed and tie me up, before handing me over to a crazy whip-wielding criminal who bears a grudge because I shot him in the balls.'

'No bother at all,' Marion said, laughing at the joke but then looking worried. 'Seriously though?'

'Obviously I'm scared,' Robin admitted.

'Knock, knock, it's Will Scarlock!' Will rhymed, as his head popped through from the main tent. 'Can you two step in for a chat?'

As Robin and Marion entered the command tent, they found Indio and Will's wife Emma waiting for them.

'If your ears were burning, it's because we've been talking about you,' Will said. 'We have a big problem.'

'Tell me something I don't know,' Robin sighed.

'We keep this mall pretty secure,' Will said, 'but I don't have an army and it's a huge space. Dozens of entrances, a hundred-and-seventy shops, plus alleyways, sewers, etcetera, etcetera. It's impossible to defend against a determined attacker.'

'Plenty of hiding places though,' Robin noted.

'We thought about that,' Indio said. 'But you'd hate being cooped up 24/7, and there's a better solution.'

'I help to run a project in the Eastern Delta,' Emma explained.

'Swampland?' Marion queried.

Emma nodded. 'The delta is where most of the refugees who end up in Sherwood Forest arrive in small boats. My project distributes aid packages to new arrivals. Maps, food, space blankets, tents. I know a lot of good people in the delta, and nobody will be looking for you out there.'

'Especially if we keep up the impression that you're still here at the mall,' Will added. 'We might even be able to lure Gisborne's new pals into a trap.'

'Makes sense,' Robin said warily. 'How long for?'

Will shrugged. 'However long it takes to get this posse off your back.'

Robin felt a touch sad. 'I know everyone here now,' he said. 'And Sheila needs help with the chickens.'

Marion laughed. 'You *constantly* moan about getting up to feed the chickens.'

'They've grown on me,' Robin admitted.

'Parts of the delta are nice in the summer,' Emma said. 'There's jet skis and fan boats. Great fishing, even a few beaches.'

'I'll do whatever you think is best,' Robin agreed.

'Marion,' Indio said, staring seriously at her daughter, 'we're absolutely not kicking you out, and you can stay here if you want, but –'

Marion cracked a huge smile. 'I *actually* get to do something interesting for once?'

Everyone laughed as Indio finished what she was going to say. 'It's going to be tough here, with the hottest time of year and Karma's baby coming in a few weeks.

I've discussed it with your father. You can keep Robin company, and we think a summer break would be good for you.'

'Totally going!' Marion said, as she did a little dance. 'I've never seen a beach!'

Robin smiled, because hiding out might even be fun with Marion coming along.

'When will we leave?' Robin asked.

'Sooner the better,' Will said.

'Neo and I are planning to set off when it starts getting dark,' Emma said. 'We'll hike out to Old Road, where some comrades are meeting us with a supply truck.'

'I'll send a couple of armed guards out to the truck with you,' Will added. 'They'll keep you safe, and they can carry extra gear, since you're gonna be away for a while.'

'Make sure you allow plenty of time, because Robin can't handle the forest,' Marion said.

Robin gave her a dirty look but didn't rise to her comment.

'You two better go pack,' Indio said.

'No fuss, no goodbyes,' Will added firmly. 'I want Robin two hundred kilometres from here before anyone else knows he's gone.'

As Indio and Marion left the tent, Will called Robin back and slid a container from under his desk. Robin grinned when he recognised a box of twenty-four Eagle-brand carbon-core arrows.

'Heard you were running low,' Will said. 'And you're thirteen soon, so consider it an early birthday present.'

'Amazing!' Robin said, grinning. 'I've never shot this brand, but they're supposed to be *really* good.'

'I had the devil's job getting them,' Will said. 'Archery equipment is sold out everywhere. It seems every kid in the land wants to be like Robin Hood.'

Emma laughed in the background, but she noticed that Robin looked a touch sad as he picked the arrows up.

'Everyone here's been really nice to me,' Robin said. 'I'm sorry for all the hassle I've caused you.'

'You won't be away for long,' Will said, smiling fondly. 'And you're a pain in the arse, Robin Hood, but we'll miss having you around.'

Look out for

JET SKIS, SWAMPS AND SMUGGLERS

Read on for an extract ...

8. DOUBLE CHOC MAGNUMS

It was after seven, but at this time of year it would stay light for hours.

Diogo had a workshop for his motorbikes in a metal shed, just off the littered beach. Marion had wheeled out and fuelled two mangled but powerful dirt bikes, being extra careful not to scrape Diogo's monstrous chromed Harley Davidson, or his collection of classic Japanese racing bikes.

'I've been waiting here like a lemon for ten minutes,' she complained, as Robin clambered through the holiday-village fence holding a tangle of metal and melted plastic. 'What the heck is that?'

'Police drone came down earlier,' Robin explained as he closed in. 'I told you I was going to look for it. I had a rough idea where it crashed, but I had to walk further than I'd thought.'

Marion studied the wreckage as Robin put it inside the bike shed. 'It's junk,' she noted.

'Interesting junk,' Robin said. 'I want to see what tech these things pack. I might even be able to work out the frequencies they transmit on.'

Marion smiled fondly. 'Such a geek.'

'Geek and proud,' Robin said. 'It's probably burnt out, but you never know. I like playing around with tech stuff, and I've not got much on when you're out on *Water Rat* with Diogo.'

'Whatever,' Marion said, checking the time on her phone. 'I've filled both bikes with petrol. Your helmet's hanging by the door. And I grabbed this for you on the way out of The Station.'

Robin looked baffled as she tossed him a rolled-up raincoat.

'Check the sky.'

'Good thinking,' he said, as he clocked a sunny evening in one direction, but ominous hammerhead clouds closing from across the water.

He stuffed the waterproof down his backpack and put on his helmet, by which time Marion had kick-started and buzzed away.

The only road leading from The Station to the rest of civilisation wound along the delta's southern edge for five kilometres. Cutting through the holiday village halved that distance, so after a few hundred metres Marion flung her bike left and sliced expertly through a gap in the wire fencing. She didn't slow down, but Robin was a less experienced rider and used his brakes.

By the time he was back up to speed, Marion was blasting over dry weeds between the lines of alpine-style chalets that once housed holidaying families. After a sharp turn they came to the empty bowl of a giant outdoor leisure pool.

They both juddered down steps at the shallow end, but as soon as Marion reached the deep end, she picked up speed, steered up a twisting water slide, then launched the bike off the platform at the top. She made a jarring landing on her front wheel but kept upright.

Robin considered the stunt as the end of the pool closed in, but he twisted his brake and stopped with his front wheel at the base of the faded blue ramp. The fact was, he'd been riding dirt bikes for a few months, while Marion's dad was a biker who'd put her on two wheels as soon as she could walk.

After pushing backwards, Robin rode a circle of shame and exited the pool via the kiddies' paddling area. Marion was waiting with a smug expression, and Robin thought she looked ridiculously cool, sat astride the bike with sun catching her black helmet and hair trailing out down her back.

'That jump was internet-worthy,' Robin said, flipping up his visor as he pulled alongside.

'I assumed you'd ride along the edge,' Marion said. 'Almost gave me a heart attack when I thought you were gonna copy me.'

'Probably would have died,' Robin admitted.

Marion laughed. 'Stick to climbing and archery – and being a geek – and leave the bike stuff to me.'

Robert Muchamore's books have sold 15 million copies in over 30 countries, been translated into 24 languages and been number-one bestsellers in eight countries including the UK, France, Germany, Australia and New Zealand.

Find out more at
muchamore.com

Follow Robert
on Facebook and Twitter
@RobertMuchamore

Discover more books and sign up to the Robert Muchamore mailing list at muchamore.com

 muchamore

 muchamorerobert

 @robertmuchamore

Thank you for choosing a Hot Key book.

If you want to know more about our authors and what we publish, you can find us online.

You can start at our website

www.hotkeybooks.com

And you can also find us on:

We hope to see you soon!